RIDDLE

Also by Dan Sherman
THE MOLE

RIDDLE

by Dan Sherman

ARBOR HOUSE   New York

Copyright ©1977 by Dan Sherman

All rights reserved, including the right of reproduction in whole or in part in any form. Published in the United States by Arbor House Publishing Company and in Canada by Clarke, Irwin & Company, Inc.

Library of Congress Catalogue Card Number: 77-79527

ISBN: 0-87795-164-0

Manufactured in the United States of America

For Nancy and Ruth

"Mirrors should reflect a little before throwing back images."

—JEAN COCTEAU

Chapter 1

IN the end there was only sand and rock. From horizon to horizon, white sand and black volcanic rock. Somewhere beyond the sloping earth was Route 66, and that led to Barstow and Lancaster, then into California's Central Valley, and finally to the big cities. There were gas stations every few miles along the route, Foster Freezes and a Howard Johnson's. But where Jimbo saw the jet go down there was only sand and rock. That was why there were no survivors. When the plane started skidding across the desert, the jagged rock tore into its belly like a razor, and the wake of sparks mixed with the fuel and the thing went up in the midnight sky like "a belch from the mouth of hell." That was how Ethel put it. She saw the pillar of flame from the window of the old trailer. But by the time Jimbo got out of bed there was only a glowing halo on the black sea of rock.

Jimbo, Ethel and the two kids scampered out to the wreck shortly before dawn. The main body of the plane was almost too hot to touch, but Jimbo said they had better not wait. In the light they might be seen, and by eleven the rock gets so hot it would fry an egg. "If there's anything good that's been scattered around, anything that's plastic, a suitcase or a hairbrush or something like that, it'll get melted," he told her.

As it was, there was very little that was plastic, the philosopher's stone of a middle class alchemy—the passengers who died that night on the desert's flat black rock were anything but middle class.

"Real" money, which as the Chinese proverb advises can only be ancient wealth, is the most permanent vessel of power. Nor was Fitzgerald talking to Hemingway about any local neighborhood millionaire, some enterprising short-order cook who happened to make a fortune in a hamburger chain, when he said the rich were very different. No lucky lumpenproletariats here. The real wealthy are more than financial statistics. They are the isolated genteel, the haute culture, the sentient lords of P.T. Barnum's myriad suckers. They are America's ruling class, and what makes them different is, they know it.

There was a time when J. P. Morgan could stop a panic on Wall Street with a phone call—or start one. In fact, it was a Morgan partner who told Giannini, the San Francisco banking king, "Right or wrong, you do as you're told on Wall Street." When FDR began to flex his federal muscles the ruling class became less vocal, but they still kept that big stick under their Carr, Son & Woor coat. Or as Jonathan Riddle, the canonical head of the Riddle empire put it, "If I exercise more influence than the average man, it's only because I've got more to lose."

In the end Jonathan Riddle lost a good deal.

Jimbo, Ethel and the kids scuttled over the black rocks, descending on the wreckage like crabs. Pockets of burning debris sent curls of smoke twisting up like blue scarves in the first bleak glimmerings of morning light. As dawn broke, the plain of rock turned to purple glass, and the hull of the jet glistened like the silver skin of a gutted fish. They were at it for hours, climbing in and out of the tail section, poking and rummaging, pulling rings off fingers, watches from wrists, shoes from feet. One of the bodies had been thrown clear and Jimbo stripped it of the softest cream flannels he had ever seen. Ethel found a string of pearls, and Jimbo a pair of blue velvet slippers with his very own initials: J.R.

When it was done Jimbo hitched the trailer to the Ford. He had never had such wealth before, and he believed that only miles of desert would protect him from those who might take it away.

Chapter 2

THE instinct for the preservation of wealth that drove Jimbo and his family further into the desert after their night of looting wasn't so different from the one that has driven lords to retire to their castles, gnomes to the center of the earth, squirrels to hide their nuts, dogs to bury their bones. Great wealth tends to spawn great walls.

A few miles outside of Boston, where the hills roll in like great green waves, and the forests brood in the dingles like some forgotten land, stands the complex of Riddle estates. Riddle homes were all over the world: Mexico, California, France, Switzerland, England, Morocco. But this was the formal seat of family power, their very own desert. The place had always been called "Swan's Way," some contended after the neighboring village while others said it was after the novel by Proust. This latter belief was dubious because the estate's founder, Andrew Riddle, never read a book in his life, except of course the Bible, and he didn't so much read as digest it. Nevertheless, old Andrew made copious amounts of money, and if nothing else, Swan's Way was a prodigious spread.

The grounds consisted of some three thousand acres (only about a thousand less than the Rockefeller estate). There were maintenance compounds, quarters for the staff, tennis courts, artificial lakes, swimming pools, houses that no one used and retreats that had been forgotten by all but the gardeners. There was also the main house, Swan's Way proper.

Supposedly the main house had forty rooms, which didn't include broom closets, bathrooms and boudoirs. However no one was really sure if forty was the correct number, because the art of counting rooms had been lost. But whether it was forty or forty-three or even fifty really didn't matter. The place was too big to be controlled by any but the staff.

Architecturally, the estate squatted on the border of bad taste. It was a sort of bastard Georgian affair that looked like something out of *The Fall of the House of Usher,* filled with dour portraits done in that grim 19th-century realism that made every model look constipated. There were also landscapes: "Sheffield in the Twilight," "Kent in the Twilight," "The Hills of Virginia," also in the twilight. It was as if the sun never shined.

Like the opening scenes of a Gothic drama, there was a distinct and calculated impression received by any visitor to the house which began while winding up the long drive. An approaching car would drop into a tiny vale, rise slowly out, swing around a wall of hedges and then . . . bang! Swan's Way. Built on a rise, the house spilled over the land like some massive sleeping dragon. Faces of the muses, faintly smiling at family secrets, had been cut into the capitals of Corinthian columns. Stern sages looked down from a projecting ledge above the huge oak doors of the main entrance. Acanthus leaves sprang from supporting corbels. Gray stone and leaded glass. The front steps would carry an army to the door, and they were low and lined with a balustrade like the steps to a museum.

It was also a place to inspire bad dreams. It had been known to frighten children, and even Andrew's first wife, Jane Riddle, once an actress from London, hated the place. But still it remained the official seat of family power. For three months of the year the main of the Riddles gathered at Swan's Way. Like his father, Jonathan held court to aunts and uncles, first cousins and second cousins. Children that he hardly knew, and the friends of children that he did not know at all, spent their summers at Swan's Way. There were houses for everyone, houses to live in, and houses to get lost in.

And now, like cripples to a shrine, the family flocked to Swan's Way. It seemed the only fitting place to be now that Jonathan Riddle was dead.

Dead. Jonathan Riddle was really dead. His fabulous Lear Jet smashed to bits all over the Western Nevada desert. His wife Linda burned, as they say, to a cinder. His pilot, co-pilot, Marge the stewardess, two assistants from the West Coast Chemical Company, Mr. Sax, the Beverly Hills accountant, Mr. Sax's secretary . . . all dead.

The plane had come in low, skidded like lightning across the cold black volcanic rock, with everyone bouncing off the walls. The belly had split open and the bodies flew out and rolled across the rocks. A miscreant family, descendants of failed goldrushers, evangelists who sold tonics and trinkets along Route 66, came out of the hills and stripped the wreck. All of Mr. and Mrs. Riddle's lovely effects that were scattered over the desert, all the watches and rings, cufflinks and shoes. Everything was now either gone or dead. . . .

"And about time too. A very fitting end, indeed," Uncle Maxwell Paige remarked cheerfully to himself. It was a cold bright morning, crisp as cellophane, clean as steel. Max had just been driven in from Boston after a flight from Canada. On the twenty-minute drive from the border of the estate to the main house, along the narrow, winding, black paved road where elms and willows laced branches in the sky to form a thatched green tunnel, Max had polished off half a flask of Jack Daniel's. Now, stepping from the lonely black Dorchester limousine he felt light and dapper. Jack, the Riddle driver, caught a whiff of whiskey-laden breath but his critical thoughts were silenced by a wink, Maxwell's famous wink, conspiratorial and confident. There was a time it might have melted the devil's heart or made the hanging judge reverse his sentence. It said, "The world may be going to seed, no doubt from my own transgressions, but can't we be friends?" Uncle Max's famous wink. It had once opened doors from brothels in North Africa to the homes of the Riddle family.

Uncle Max was met on the steps by Andrew Soames, the titular head of the Riddle staff. Soames was English, allegedly with Montgomery in North Africa, and he managed his charge as if he were defending Tobruk. He was a gaunt, snowy man who met the day-to-day joys and disasters with the same quiet stoicism. Politic, circumspect, meticulous, Soames would have been an attendant lord in any age. As downstairs legend had it, Soames had never been anything else than what he was now. Nor would he ever change. He did not appear to age. He would never retire.

The previous evening when the news of Jonathan Riddle came, Soames had called his immediate staff into the parlor. There had been brandy on the Queen Anne card table and thirteen blue crystal goblets with acorn baluster stems. The blinds had been drawn tight with velvet cord, and only a single yellow light was burning. When all was quiet, he announced, "The Master and Mistress are dead." Six words only, they might have been six perfectly cut diamonds held in an open palm before the dozen men and women that stood in a ragged semicircle. Soames was born for announcements like that.

When it was over the chorus of ritual sobs began, and had Soames not been so fully drenched in the moment he might have noticed that at least half his audience was secretly but quite thoroughly glad that Jonathan Riddle was dead.

In the fifteen hours between the announcement and the time Max had arrived, Soames had tuned the sepulchral note to perfection. He now ushered Max into the great hall with a dismal formality.

Uncle Max was not everyone's uncle, though that was the title he somehow had adopted. He fit spuriously into the family tree like a mutant twig. No matter how it was trimmed, poisoned or simply sheared off, when the spring rain fell like silver and the sun glittered down like gold, it would always pop out as good as new. His own family had not taken Max seriously for years. Not since he pissed away his own fortune. There had been years of aberration. There was an expedition to Tibet, and months at the feet of a Himalayan lama. He was supposed to have sunk thousands into an occult society modeled after the Golden Dawn. And finally there had been a heroic party that lasted for weeks, turning the population of a small Caribbean island into a pack of debauched sensualists.

With his father's legacy spent in a matter of a few years (no mean feat), Max took off for Havana with a Parisian cabaret singer. Stories became garbled after that. One said he spied for British Intelligence. Another said he fell madly in love with a Spanish duchess one magic summer on Cyprus, and when she snubbed him, he joined the Abraham Lincoln Brigade and fought against her father in the Spanish Civil War. Still another said he went to Africa and actually hitched up with Hemingway, or at any rate someone just like Hemingway. But however he spent those intervening years, when Linda Paige married Jonathan Riddle, Uncle Max showed up on the doorstep as bedraggled and happy as a department store Santa Claus. After pelting his sister with fistfuls of rice, he presented them with a stuffed alligator, allegedly killed with his bare hands.

For over four years after the merger of the Riddle and Paige families Max enjoyed something akin to patronage from his new brother-in-law. Within society at Swan's Way he had the freedom of a jester and the power of a minister. Young Jonathan had the family jewels laid at his feet, and Maxwell was the man who held up each glistening stone to his eye, whispering possibilities, counseling and advising. They were four happy years. There were garden parties on Sundays with lawn tables spread with thirty dozen quails' eggs, bowls of fresh mayonnaise and lobster. They chased foxes through the forests in shiny black boots and red livery, never caught them and came back laughing and sweaty. Even though Jonathan was warned of danger, told that Max was some kind of mad Rasputin who would spend his money and ruin his future, business actually thrived. Millions poured in on top of millions. Jonathan gave Max a helium balloon for his birthday and they sailed it across the river.

And then something began. Something apparently moved into the forest. Jonathan once told Max he could "feel" it at night. Some animals were found butchered in the woods. There were rumors. The days grew shorter, the nights longer—the nights were very bad. Then Africa for a rest. Then what happened in Africa. Then the long recuperation. Finally Jonathan was recovered, whereupon he all but banished Max from Swan's Way forever. Not like Jonathan, really.

For years after Max left the estate no one heard much of him. There was an occasional postcard from London or Paris or Berlin. Someone claimed to have seen him scuttling from a library in Munich, dashing down sidestreets to avoid a familiar face, lumbering with an armful of books. His letters to his sister Linda revealed nothing of himself, once he had phoned from across the Atlantic and begged her to take her son and leave Swan's Way "before it was too late." Except by that time Max's counsel meant nothing to anyone but children, and even they tended to snicker. No one had actually barred him from their homes, but beneath the angry shadow of the changed Jonathan's influence, it seemed that even the famous winking eye of Maxwell Paige had found trouble with the locks of Riddle homes. It took Jonathan's abrupt death to change that.

Max followed the stiff old figure of Soames down the hall. Family and friends, those early to arrive, Soames explained, had gathered in the little garden for coffee. "Shall I announce you now, sir?"

"Who's here? Are Eleanor and Burt here?" Max had a curious way of sniggering when he said the name of his younger sister, Eleanor.

"They are."

"Well, that's nice." Max slurred the last word.

"And shall I announce you, sir?"

"By all means, Soames. A little theater party in the garden, no?" The two men walked through a large room that was off the hall, past a bust of someone long dead and a Chippendale bureau where Dresden figurines danced behind squares of cabinet crystal.

At the end of the room a white double door led to the garden. Soames stopped, then walked into the morning light. Through the panes of glass Maxwell could see the circle of people look up from their coffee and crescent rolls. The party was seated around a blue wrought-iron table, draped with white linen and set with silver. Soames bent into the ear of an elderly woman. She nodded, and someone said, "Oh! Uncle Max, welcome!"

A blanched light sprayed through the drape of willows, lost its coarser tones and so achieved a fitting refinement. The shaded folds of Irish linen, the glint off the silver, the contrasting black of crinoline, these were also fitting. Fitting, Max thought, rolling the word in his head as he stepped down the garden path. A very good painter might have captured the scene, a question of brushing subtlety on top of subtlety until the vulgarity emerged.

Half a dozen men and women bobbed like worker bees around Aunt Stella. She sat on cushions laid against a high-back vine of wrought iron. Quiet sighs and cramped whispers.

Stella Riddle was Jonathan's aunt, his father's sister. Ever since the death of Jonathan's parents, Stella had really been the first lady of the house. That was, not officially the head, because there had been his wife Linda, but Linda was . . . well, of course the Paiges were a quality family, but still Linda was not really suited for Swan's Way, especially after what happened to Jonathan in Africa. At any rate, that was the understanding. And now that Jonathan was dead it seemed that Aunt Stella had jumped on the coach and taken the reins, at least temporarily. At least until *he* could be found, and it was determined one way or another just what *he* wanted to do. "He" being the prodigal, uncontrollable son and heir, Jamie Riddle.

Max slipped into the chair next to Stella. She smiled at him like the old grey fox that she was. When a waiter in a white tunic with a black armband leaned over his shoulder, Max said, "Yes coffee, but why don't you put a spot of brandy in it?" His sister, Eleanor, fired him a dirty look. Max ignored her.

Max and Eleanor seemed nothing like brother and sister. Where he was round and fair, with eyes like blue Christmas lights, she was thin and dark. When young she had been beautiful, in a lean sort of way; now she was gracious. She had large features, like an exquisite clown. Linda had had the same, and whenever Max saw Eleanor, which was usually for only a few days every year, the first thing he'd look for was the thin scar that ran across her chin. Barely perceptible, it had been the start of their falling out. Eleanor had been eight, Max twelve. He had swung the rope. One end had been tied to an acorn tree. She jumped. "Up and down, up and down all bloody afternoon," Max would say. "Then once she goes up and comes down . . . thump! Six dinky stitches and the woman has never forgiven me."

Those who knew the story and their relationship claimed that "hate" was too strong a word. "All right then," Max would counter. "Eleanor loves me with a dismal effort."

Things had become worse when Eleanor married Burt Hoskins, the son of a plumbing magnate from Kansas who, although he got a nice little packet from his father, was considered by everyone to have married Eleanor for her money. Max, however, was the only one gauche enough to talk about it.

Burt was a once-herculean figure who had lost his trim. His hair was thinning. His chin was beginning to double. He stood flanked now by Stella and Eleanor, balancing a fragile saucer in the palm of one hand while holding the cup between thumb and forefinger of the other.

"It was good of you to come, Max," he said nervously.

"Good of us all to come," Max returned. Fight lies with lies would be his policy.

"How long are you intending to stay?" Eleanor cut in, and Burt dropped his head and raised his eyebrows to add weight.

"That, I suppose, depends . . ." Max paused, ". . . on certain circumstances."

"Well, Burt has a sales meeting in Detroit on the tenth," Eleanor offered, perhaps implying that normal people have reliable and generally controllable schedules.

"Is that still plumbing that we're mucking about with?"

"Western Manufacturers Association," Burt said, nodding. "But I'm prepared to forgo the convention if the family needs me. That is, it's a difficult time. If things don't really smooth out, if events happen that need attention, then I'll cancel." Burt was not really speaking to Max. This was directed to the others, Eleanor and Stella particularly. This was their pact against Max. It was also, Max believed, a pact against Jamie. Max understood. He knew how they felt, what they believed, what they feared. Years ago he might have been upset by it. He might have told them they were selfish and greedy and blind, that they had completely missed the real issue. Now he could only view these pacts with tolerance. Twenty years staring in the face of a resident horror, and they still didn't see it.

Among all of the Riddle circle, the family, the friends, the staff, there were only two who had always accepted Max on his own terms. First there was Carry, Burt and Eleanor's adopted daughter. The beautiful imp, Carry. She wasn't really a Paige at all. She had been taken in after the "African Tragedy," and so she too was obliquely part of Jonathan's fall, and essentially an outsider. Then there was *him*, son Jamie Riddle. Like Max and Carry, he too was an outsider, but an outsider by choice.

They didn't want to talk about *him*. Not anyone who sat around the table in the garden. But Max was feeling bolder now. He was well on his way to being pleasantly high. Not drunk, just high, and he liked it. So with the authority of half a flask of whiskey, and now the brandy, Max began to speak about Jamie.

"I should think that Carry will be just delighted to see him. I seem to recall they were the best of friends. Tight as thieves. Oh, when was it? Eleanor, you remember, don't you?"

"Remember what?"

"Well, perhaps you weren't there, but Stella was." Max was one of the few with enough years behind him, or enough cheek, to call Stella by name. For everyone else it was Mrs. Riddle. "Remember . . ." and he hung on the word as if he were a circus fortune teller about to reveal something terrible . . . "Remember the time Jonathan caught them swimming in the lake down by the golf course. It wasn't really a lake, it was the golf course hazard, filled with green muck and your balls." He pointed to Burt.

"I remember," Stella said in her voice that raked words over gravel. "I remember that they hadn't any clothing on."

"Naked as damn jaybirds," Max laughed. "Oh, it was one thing after another. First Carry, and then him. Regular little outlaws. But they both turned out all right," and then drawing out the last words like a gaudy pink carnival ribbon, he spoke to them all. "Wouldn't you say?"

Chapter 3

MAX'S younger sister, Eleanor, and her husband, Burt, who barely tolerated him; Linda, an older sister who had always thought him completely insane; her husband, Jonathan Riddle, once Max's closest friend, who had all but booted him from Swan's Way: if one were to keep tally, then these were pretty grim statistics. Better to view them as fragments of broken dreams. Added to these were cousins and second cousins who said Max did not pay his debts. There were children who claimed he cheated at croquet, and young ladies who believed Max looked at them improperly. Indeed, one might have seen the man as a lonely, decrepit old bugger prowling parks after dark, searching in garbage cans for the last drop of cheap wine, or drinking Vitalis as a last resort. It hadn't, of course, come to that, not even remotely, but at the twilight of Max's life he had little of anything tangible to show. "Only a miserable bundle of years," he once confessed in a darker mood. But even that was nowhere near the truth.

The truth was that whatever had become of Uncle Maxwell Paige had nothing to do with profligate youth, nor a few outstanding debts, nor the tiny scar inflicted on Eleanor's chin. If nothing else, Max had come to know the truth. It had taken nearly twenty years to understand, and then only partially. But it was not a truth that could be carried around like photographs in a wallet. It was a secret to everyone who knew. It had to do with the fall of Jonathan, his "nervous breakdown in Africa," if that was what one euphemistically wished to call it. Max had come to believe that Jonathan suffered more than a mere "breakdown." There had been the attack on the campsite in the night. Carry's parents were killed. Jonathan had been badly hurt and, as far as Max was concerned, never recovered. So that it had not really been Jonathan who returned from Africa, not at least the Jonathan that Max had known. The man who returned from Africa was terrifying to him, beastly... never mind the grammatical euphemism—beast, was closer to it, and perhaps phantom even more so. Whatever, the Jonathan that had returned to Swan's Way seemed to Max to be enclosed in a cold wind. A chill that had swept down from the hills, had come through the corridors, room after room, blowing in on those long nights.

Although Jonathan was dead, the force that had driven him might well not be. If it came round again, it would come to possess Jonathan's son Jamie. Max, not without reason, was sure of it. . . .

As the day wore on there were more arrivals. Riddle cousins that Max hardly knew, handfuls of Riddle friends that he didn't want to know. There were quiet hellos and little kisses all about the garden. Stella received condolences like debts. The staff floated in and out of the hedgerows, whispering into ears, then beelining back to the kitchens. By late afternoon the visitors retired to guest houses like members of a monastic convention off to meditate. Max knew they were going to talk about *him*, Jamie. It was like an unspoken premonition. They all had it. Jonathan's aunts and uncles, cousins and friends. No one had mentioned the name, but it was perfectly clear. They believed *he* was going to return. "And they're sweating," Max grinned. "They're sweating like voodoo victims." All except Carry.

When Max found out that his adopted niece had also come to Swan's Way, he rushed off to find her. He checked her bedroom in the main house, but she was not there. "I should think Miss Caroline would be with the others in the garden," Soames had said. She wasn't, and Max went on for almost an hour before he found her with a bottle of sherry in the summer tea room down by the brook.

She was sitting on the window seat. A glass dangling from the finger of one hand. He entered from behind her and she didn't see him. For a moment he simply stared. She was a thin figure with blond hair like a ragged halo that dribbled to her shoulders. Her eyes were green or, in another light, grey, the lashes long and dark. She had a child's nose, and the face too was round and firm, the cheekbones high. While her mouth, Max had always thought with amusement and pleasure, curved like a dolphin's, a knowing dolphin with a slow mischievous smile. She was wearing a black silk dress with a print of tiny mauve flowers. She had taken her shoes off, and one tanned leg was propped in the branches of a rubber plant. Max held the vision for a second, watched her stub a cigarette out in the soil of a potted fern, and then, "Hello, baby."

"Uncle Max!" She ran to him, and gave him a kiss that might have been reserved for her father.

Max had been there when Eleanor and Burt Hoskins had taken Carry in. She had been about two then, and when his younger sister held Carry to her shoulder, the little girl fought for dear life. She screamed, "Mommy . . . mommy!" But her parents were already dead by then, that awful nightmare in Africa with Jonathan, but really, wasn't the child fortunate? After all, her real parents had been stony broke, while Burt and Eleanor were more than merely set up.

Max knew what his sister had been thinking. She wanted a nice little girl who would curtsy for relatives, a little girl who could be packed off to school with kisses and chocolates, a daughter she could take to Central Park on Wednesdays through the 76th Street entrance (Wednesdays were the nannies' days off, so all the mothers met on Wednesdays. No one would be caught dead at the park on a Friday or a Monday). Eleanor wanted a girl who would grow up and go to Vassar and properly flirt with all those wealthy young preppies from Choate or St. Pauls. In short, Eleanor wanted a little girl who would be just like she had been, a little girl who would not only pay for her keep, but make a profit as well. What she got, though, was Carry, a little girl after Max's own heart.

It was really just Carry Weatherton, because formal adoption papers were never drawn up. Most people called her Hoskins, although she preferred Weatherton. But either way she grew up to be as pretty as sin, and broke the richest hearts in Derfield. That would have been fine in Eleanor's mind, but she broke them the wrong way. She broke them with a playful maliciousness that said, "You may be the son of the world's largest douche bag manufacturer, but to me you're just another arrogant horny jerk." What was worse was that where the other girls only flirted, Carry went romping off to bed. That was supposed to give a girl a bad reputation, and it did, but only with the girls. The boys flocked to her like puppy dogs, wide-eyed, salivating. At least half of them asked for marriage. When it came time for most girls to begin looking seriously, Carry ran off with a guitar player from London who grossed more money a year than a third of the Derfield families. She stayed with the musician through one tour, and then she had been reminded of her childhood love all over again.

Carry had been living in a chateau in the south of France, spending her days lying naked on the rooftop, reading Mark Twain, drawing tiny rodents like E.M. Escher's. Her lover was teaching her to play the guitar. She had no talent, but he bought her a beautiful green one with mother-of-pearl inlay on the frets and bumblebees painted on the body. In the evenings they would go gambling, although Carry preferred to trundle down to the clubs and listen to the gossip: money, politics, occasionally stories of crime.

It happened about a week after the Arab terrorists murdered

the Israeli athletes. There had been talk about reprisals, mostly from two drunken men in St. Laurent evening jackets. They claimed they were importers, and sat down with Carry and her lover to sell them Navajo bracelets. The goods were genuine, but probably stolen. Carry's lover declined, but bought them a few drinks. The talk turned from Indians to espionage, and the two importers, particularly the dark young one, began speaking with bragging authority.

Carry was listening with sleepy indifference, dipping a finger in a glass of burgundy, tracing a mosaic of hummingbirds on the table. Then she heard it, just one word. It had been slipped into a rapid exchange. For Carry it was the first signpost in years, a spark of light on the horizon. One of those importers had mentioned *his* name.

"In connection with what?" Max said from where he sat on a corner of the window seat.

"I'm not really sure. This man had been describing someone to Graham, that was my friend. He had been describing a soldier, but he used the French, so it wasn't exactly a soldier, but more an assassin. He said he had heard this assassin would be used by the Israelis for revenge. I'm not sure of the details, neither Graham nor I had been paying close attention. Afterwards I asked the importers about him, but it was as if they had already said too much."

"How did they say it?"

"Riddle, that's all."

"You might have misunderstood. Perhaps it was 'riddle' as in mystery, or enigma. You know, like the Riddle of the Sphinx."

"No, Max. I heard it. I was sure. That man was talking about Jamie."

"Jamie." Max sighed. It was true, Carry would know that he was near again from just hearing his name. She would be the only one who might be able to see him clearly, even through all those tears. And the way she had spoken it, breathed it like a whisper. Keep it a secret, she might have said. Because after all, hadn't they had many secrets together?

"It wasn't how I had expected it would happen," Carry continued.

Max had the thought that she should have said "dreamed" instead of "expected."

"You know, I could see him calling me," she said. "I'd pick up the phone one day, and say, 'Hello.' Then he would say, 'Hello, it's me.' But the way it happened, there was something so absurdly seedy about it. This dark balding drunk letting Jamie's name dribble out, it was funny. I mean funny weird, not funny ha ha."

"How long ago was this?"

"Three months."

"Did you try to find out any more?"

"Not really. I asked around a bit, but nothing came. And after these years of waiting I thought, 'This is a sign that we'll meet, and that's enough.' Then came the plane crash, and now I'm here."

"You believe he'll come back, don't you?" Carry nodded over the glass of sherry. Max caught it from the corner of his eye and turned his face to the window. From where he sat there was a long view of the grounds. Past a curtain of drooping willow leaves, he saw the slope of the lawns, a bit of white sandstone and finally the parade of trees like a rank of soldiers guarding the edge of the forest.

Jamie and Carry, the two of them used to play in that forest, Max remembered. Once, he knew for certain, they had made love there. It had been Jamie's sixteenth birthday, and Carry had led him into the forest, and on a bed of red leaves they had made love. It had been the first time for both of them. Max now realized that they had never really gotten over it.

"So you're like two wolves," Max said, capping the thought. Carry laughed self-consciously, and told him to shut up. But Max felt that was because "wolves" had been such an appropriate image. She told him he was drunk, which was true, and he smiled, but still the image of wolves stayed there. Two wolves poised on distant mountains, separated for years and still remembering one another, preserving themselves for each other. He liked that vision. It was a little maudlin, but Carry was right, he was drunk, and he kept seeing those two lonely wolves. . . . They had grown up together, two small frightened souls with a pact against the world. Wolves . . . it was particularly applicable to Jamie. After all, it was Jamie who finally chewed through the ropes and started slashing away at everyone. Well, perhaps not exactly slashing, but certainly there had been some angry bites.

"It's been years," Carry sighed, finishing something that Max had missed. "I'm sure we'll both seem very different to one another." But Max knew she didn't really believe that. All that had changed was that they'd grown up. Jamie would have bigger teeth now, fangs no doubt. It would be wonderful if he came back with fangs. He might need them. If his father had had fangs, it might never have begun in the first place. Max's old friend Jonathan might never have fallen, become what he became, if *he* had had fangs.

Chapter 4

WERE Aunt Stella, or Eleanor, or any of the others to have seen the only son of Mr. Jonathan Riddle as he had been, say, four days ago their worst fears would have been substantiated. Radan had sent Jamie Riddle under the Egyptian wires to spike a terrorist, or put him to the torch. But the run had blown at the border. What had begun as a vague apprehension, an uneasy feeling that there was someone behind, nearly ended in a full-blown flap. And so Riddle sat six days in a matchbox room, breathless and haunted, high above the clammering, ringing one thousand three hundred years of yellow-washed squalor that was Cairo.

And if Stella, or Eleanor or any of that crew were to have seen him, straining for a footfall on the stairs below, or hovering at the window watching the streets for signs of the secret police, they would have concluded that even the sons of the very rich could fall to the gutters.

Jamie Riddle had not really fallen into the gutters. He had

fallen in with an Israeli paramilitary organization, and so if he was a dog of war at least he was only fed by a single hand.

Or beaten, as it had seemed, when he squatted on his haunches in the corner of the Cairo flat. Marking time with the voice of the muezzin that called the faithful to pray, he spent hours wondering what had gone wrong with the run. Or later, when the panic had begun to sag to boredom, he watched a family of red ants grow fat on poison they had built a resistance to generations before.

In the end he had decided he would kill one ant a day as a kind of sacrifice until somebody came and got him out. But God in His mercy, watching out for all His creatures, sent Toby Sachs with two blank passports like lambs to Abraham.

At the time Riddle thought his old friend Toby a poor choice to fish him out of Cairo. Sachs was a twenty-seven-year-old Moroccan Jew, and although he had been educated in America and spoke like the son of a New York garment executive, he had one of those lean Zionist faces that the Jewish Defense League displayed on posters to represent the indomitable strength of Israeli armies. With red hair and freckles he looked nothing like an Arab, and so the two had to saunter out of Egypt as British students, about the flimsiest cover imaginable.

"At least I look like an Aryan," Riddle had whispered as they stood in line at Egyptian customs. That was true. He had small, delicate almost feminine features, a narrow nose and fair hair.

"Not just an Aryan, asshole," Toby had countered, "you look like a fucking Nazi." But if Riddle looked like a Nazi, it was a Nazi gone to seed. If there was strength it seemed undisciplined, if there was power it seemed unchanneled. Actually nothing could have been further from the mark, but the first impression had frequently worked to his advantage.

Toby had read about the death of Jonathan Riddle enroute to Jamie's rescue, but he waited until Jamie had been debriefed by Radan before telling him. Initially Riddle had not been particularly upset. But as time went on or, more exactly, after his private talk with Radan, he became morose. For the first time since Toby had known him, Riddle was indecisive. One moment he was fully resolved to return to America and "pick up the pieces," and in another he complained that he needed more time to think it out. Hence the cafe in which they now sat waiting until some girl Jamie was to meet came and took him away for the weekend. Hence the drinks, one after another. Hence the long periods of silence.

The day was clear with that watery afternoon light that had been captured so well by the Impressionists. The two men sat at the blue wooden table beneath a Cinzano umbrella. Gusts of wind skittered along the Seine, tossing up ripples of chop, whipping the tasseled umbrella ends into tight little frenzies. They were trapped in the unfulfilled silence that often proceeds confession. There were things that needed to be said.

It was Riddle who spoke first. "So, I've decided, Toby." He was staring into an iridescent whirlpool of oil slick on the water.

"Yeah, well, I thought you had. When are you leaving?"

"Monday, Tuesday. Whenever I can get a flight out." The concentric rings of oil were like a spell, holding him rigid.

"I was going to get a room at the Montmartre for a few days. Eric will be around. If you want to see Eric you can come by."

Their voices were clipped and cold. Napoleon's farewell to the Old Guard.

"Who are you going off with for the weekend?"

"Just some friend."

"Who is she?" Toby was smiling for the first time. "It's that chick you met the other day, isn't it? What's her name? Candy?"

"Yes, Candy."

"I can't believe that you're that horny, going off with some chick named Candy." And then leaning forward, leveling the sarcastic grin, "What's her last name?"

It was ridiculous and Riddle said nothing, which condemned them to another silence.

The last light of day was streaking up the river, turning the tiny waves of windy chop to silver and gold. A bell began to toll the hour and a flight of gulls came wheeling from the flourished eave of gothic gray stone.

Toby turned his head with the sweep of birds and let his words drift out like bubbles to the wind. "I meant to ask you. I mean, I was curious about what he said to you the other day."

"Radan?"
"Yeah."
Riddle chewed on the end of a toothpick. "Nothing."
"Come on, man. The old man never says nothing."
"All right, he asked about the run. He wanted to know what went down. There was the usual cosmic bullshit." Riddle's laconic cynicism again. Toby remembered it as a survival from a younger Jamie, a tough-talking punk, hardly more than a marvelous street fighter, mean and shabby as an alley cat. Then he caught a sudden vision of Jamie sitting on the bed of a squalid London flat. The door was splintered from where he had been throwing a switchblade. "What did you tell him?"
"What could I say? I was blown. I'm in two days. I make contact with the Turk. I'm about to go back with some stick, and suddenly the whole fucking army is on my ass."
Actually there was more. Riddle had felt himself haunted . . . yes, melodramatic as it sounded, the word was right . . . haunted by the presence of some shadow from the moment he crossed the border. Someone apparently had been on him from the start. He simply knew it. Radan had been particularly interested in those early premonitions.
"What about when you told him about your parents, that you might be leaving? No gold watch? No blessing? He didn't ask you to kiss his beard?"
"He told me not to write." Which was not the truth, but now Riddle sat frowning into the face of an image—the ragged bent figure of Radan. It was enough to frighten anyone, and certainly deny explanations. Radan was like a dark ghoul from the Old Testament, a mystic from the desert, with sand in his shoes and stars in his beard. He'd once told Riddle that intensity properly channeled was a ladder to heaven. He claimed his ladder had been hate and revenge.
"He told me," Riddle finally began, "he told me that if I had to go, then go."
"Just like that?"
"What's he supposed to say?"
"I don't know. It just seems that you went a long way to end it like that."

"Is that what they say? That I went a long way with Radan?"

"Some say that, Jamie. Some of us who've seen you work, Jamie, would have to say that you went pretty damn far."

Toby turned his head away, and popped a cigarette in his mouth. He lit a match, but the wind snuffed it out, and he sat goading Riddle with a sad profile, his eyes blinking, the cigarette kicking in the wind.

Well, whatever they had said, Riddle still cared for his friends. "I'm not condemning him, Tob. It's just that, well, you know how Radan is. You ask him the time of day and he'll give you some Kabalistic bullshit about how there is no time. The guy believes that radios work because there are little men inside them."

"That's real funny, Jamie," Toby said. "Has that always been your attitude? Because that's pretty fucked."

"No. It hasn't always been my attitude."

"Well, then what's changed?"

What had changed with Jamie Riddle was that when he had come to Radan he had simply been another bitter rebel who had yanked out the silver spoon he was born with and sharpened it to a cutting edge. Maybe he had slashed the tires on a Rolls-Royce, ground his name into the finish and stolen the hub-caps, but he had never done much more than raise a few eyebrows in high circles. An annoyance, nothing the insurance wouldn't cover. Radan, on the other hand, had taught him that even a spoon, if one knew how to use it, could take out a man's throat.

"What's changed, Toby, is that I've begun to wonder about things."

"What things?"

"I don't know." He paused and shook his head. "I'm not sure what the point has been."

"The point of what?"

"What I've become."

"You mean with Radan?"

"Yes, I mean with Radan."

"Well, you're damn good at what you do—"

"Which means?"

"Which means just that."

"Well, it damn well *better* mean more than that."

Toby winced, took the cigarette from his mouth. It broke in his fingers. Just then they might have been two lost students, existential refugees from the Left Bank... Toby slouched over the table staring into the twisting yellow swirls of Pernod, Riddle leaning back on the wrought-iron chair, a bit seedy in green corduroy, a silk shirt with loose cuffs and a silver bangle on his wrist.

"I'll tell you what Radan said to me," Riddle finally said. He owed this much. "Radan told me that I hadn't gone far enough down the road with him. He said that he'd failed me, he said that he'd let me work myself into a corner that demanded an enemy and I didn't have the strength to fight it."

"He said it like that?"

"In so many words."

"That's an odd thing for him to say. I mean that's the opposite of what one would expect."

"You think so?"

"Come on, Jamie, you know what I'm talking about."

"No, I don't know what you're talking about."

'All right. Point of fact, you became the best, didn't you?"

"That depends on what you mean by the best."

"Christ, Jamie! What do you want to hear?"

"Well, I'm not all that proud of it."

"I don't think that was part of the deal. No one asked or expected you to be proud of it. You did what you were supposed to do. You did goddamn good."

"But that's the point. Did I do so good? I don't mean was I proficient at what I did, but literally, was it good?"

"I don't know what you mean."

"Don't you Toby? Haven't you ever wondered?"

"No, man. I don't know what you're talking about."

"Then tell me, Tob, how did Radan describe the targets? He used to call them evil, didn't he? Unmitigated evil, right?"

"Yeah, well, I heard him use that term before."

"He'd say, 'Remember, Jamie, there's evil out there, unmitigated evil.' He'd tell me that I had to be tough. Well, you know what tough means in his dictionary? How about vicious? And he was serious. Well, that was fine, because some of those targets were real bastards, but I'll tell you something, Tob. There were times when I was so good at it, so fucking good that it was scary. You understand what I'm saying? You can be hunting down a Hitler but still there are moments when you wonder, is this guy worse than I am? Am I better, just because I'm stronger? You tell that to the real victims. So when Radan tells me that I haven't gone far enough down his road, don't you think I'm entitled to know just what the hell he means?"

Another burst of wind came rolling up the river like a cheering crowd. Leaves trembled in its wake and when they were still again Toby was on his feet. "It doesn't matter, Jamie. I'll see you Monday?"

"Yeah, Monday."

"Eric will want to see you before you go."

"Yeah, I'll be there."

"And don't worry, man. Radan says things. They don't need to mean anything special. Hell, it doesn't really matter what he meant. You know, the answers to those crazy kinds of things he says, they don't matter." Toby dropped a handful of coins on the table and was gone.

Toby was wrong.

Chapter 5

JAMIE, looking so cool now, watched Toby thread his way out through the tables. He ordered another glass of house wine, lit up a cigarette and settled into the wait, like an animal on its haunches at the mouth of a cave. His cave was memory and quiet time.

He hadn't always been cool. When he first arrived in Europe after running from Swan's Way he was only a lightweight rebel, a tough-talking punk as Toby had said. He'd been his father's son, and his father had very nearly broken him. Jonathan Riddle had taken his son, bangs in his little boy eyes and Indian Walk sandals at thirty-five dollars a pair on his feet, and had lectured and beaten on him, just as he liked to lecture and beat anyone who stood in his way. Jonathan called this form of education dressage, a word from the Old French meaning to break a horse. But Jamie was strong. When Jonathan threw him onto the floor and hit him with a riding crop, the boy found a hole and crawled into that hole and found himself in another world.

From this underground, Jamie took his pot shots.

It was this history that Radan had been referring to when he told Jamie, "You have worked yourself into a role which demands an enemy." Soldiers needed enemies. The only trouble, however, was that after Radan had turned Riddle into something truly vicious, Riddle was a bit unclear just who his enemy was supposed to be. Naturally he had his opposite numbers in Soviet and Arab intelligence, but they were simply the opposition, not really the same as a nemesis. And Radan seemed to put a lot of stock in finding a nemesis. "We all have a personal dragon," he would say. "To slay that dragon is holy." . . .

Riddle ordered another glass of the house wine. Time drifted past like the slow black barges on the Seine. Another hour gone, half a pack of Gaulois. He counted five hollow gongs of the great bell, and then many a lesser bell as they marched across Paris. It was five o'clock. That meant Candy was two hours late, which was about par for the course.

And then she was calling his name. "Jaammee!" A shrill eruption at crystal-shattering pitch. "Jaammee!" It rang of a life that Riddle had drifted through five years ago, a life of champagne brunches and oysters at midnight. "Jaammee!" It rang of slow waltzes on Mediterranean evenings, and it rang of Miss Candy d'Light.

She came sauntering through the red and white checked tablecloths, pink and curly blond with an enormous pair of pastel sunglasses falling down her nose. She kissed him on the lips and he caught a whisp of languorous grape and tonic. "Jamie, darling, I'm so sorry. So sorry that I'm late but you know how impossible it is to keep track of time in Paris . . ."

Candy d'Light was supposed to have been born with another name. Riddle had heard it was Susan Meyers from Scranton, Pennsylvania. At sixteen she was seduced in the dressing room of the local Elks Club by a Norwegian ballet dancer. She traveled with the troupe through ten states, and played handmaiden to the women and mistress to the men who didn't have their taps reversed. After eight weeks she wound up in New York married to the company patron, a fifty-year-old appliance king. She soon killed the poor man by breaking his heart and then ran off to Europe and higher circles. That was where she met young Jamie Riddle. "And then you didn't call me for three years. Or was it five? Either way it was a naughty thing to do. What could you have been doing that was so important?"

"Traveling, just traveling, that's all," Riddle muttered, a cigarette wobbling between his lips.

They had met again on the streets the day before. Candy had been running for a cab, and on the way they made plans. It had happened so fast that Riddle was a little surprised that she had come. When he told her that she laughed. "Jamie, I wouldn't have missed this for the world. I've heard you've led the most dramatic life imaginable. I've heard you were up to the most romantic adventures." She taunted him with a finger. Her nails were painted bright ochre. Then she cocked her head playfully to one side so that a silky blond curl fell to the corner of her mouth. She pulled at the hem of her mandarin-orange velvet dress, with the bodice cut low and straight across with just straps for the shoulders.

"I've heard," she said slowly, squinting at him through enormous eyelashes, "that you have been an adventurer. Is that the word? No, I don't think so. But anyway, I've heard that you were some sort of a commando in Palestine." She used the word "Palestine" instead of "Israel," Riddle imagined, because it was so coquettishly naïve. Or French, maybe. Or both.

Riddle didn't mind. Candy might be a little foolish, but if he boarded the plane for the States he would be in Boston in about twelve hours, at Swan's Way in another three, and then whatever he had buried under ten years and thousands of miles would be on him like an avalanche. Candy d'Light at least would give him a little time to prepare himself.

"And it's going to be heaven. I've got it all arranged at Michael's villa. No one but us. Just heaven." Candy scooped up Riddle's hand and pressed it to her lips. She kissed it once and was about to kiss it again when she frowned and began to examine it as if it were injured. "Jamie, what have you been doing with your hands? They're like bricks, as hard as bricks."

Chapter 6

CANDY had a blue Jaguar coupe, and when Riddle reached the outskirts of Paris he drove it for all it was worth. She told him it wasn't exactly her own car. It belonged to the son of England's Ambassador to Turkey. She was to have met him that afternoon, "But he's really such a poor old goose," she sighed. "Occasionally you'll meet a woman who's a goose, but a man ... that's just too much to bear. You know the type I mean. His trousers are always creased just so. When he sits down he picks at the crease with his thumb nail. It's something right out of a Somerset Maugham novel. He wants me to liberate him emotionally and sexually of course. That's why it's all right that I've run off with you in his wonderful auto. I mean, what better way to begin the boy's education than with a broken heart? He'll thank me for it."

Candy talked all the way. They passed a blanket of vineyards that climbed into the hills and vanished into the grey sky of dusk, and she began to talk about the wealthy wine merchants of Burgundy and the South. After the vineyards the road narrowed and plunged into the darkness of a long valley where the forest spilled to the edge of the highway. Two more hours took them into the hills, where the road became a lonely bridge over a void of black forest. Above, the stars were like a frosted net. A sultry red moon rose above the black humps of mountain, swimming through the night sky, swimming through a tangle of stars.

Riddle first noticed it as they were gliding into the high country. The road swung close to the side of a bleak rocky crag. Shadows pounced down at them. Then, like the deer that catches scent of the lion, the fear returned. Perhaps not exactly fear, because there was nothing tangible. Except Riddle had just seen the flash of headlights in the rear-view mirror, and although another car behind them was nothing to freak about, nothing logically to base fear on, still the thought that they were being followed rose in him like a surfacing shark.

On the open road, in the palm of a valley, the car was still behind them, as was Riddle's impression. And he couldn't shake it. He had had the same fear in Cairo. At first just a suspicion, an unacknowledged prescience. He had been in a crowded street. Men in cotton djellabas were milling about the souks. There were whirlwinds of sandy dust, a smell of burning meat and hot spices. Then from out of nowhere, like a terrible memory from . . . where? . . . from childhood . . . "I'm being followed." Until he had known for certain, the suspicion was like a nightmare where one knows one is sleeping but still can't escape. Ridiculous, but still . . .

In the distance the lights of great estates nodded and winked through passing foliage. Low trees seemed to writhe and then limp away in the tall grass as Riddle's headlights mowed through the countryside. Something was burning miles away. They passed a stone church ruin, rising like an enormous skull to frighten giants. Candy began to give directions. "There'll be a gate on our right . . . very soon . . . there!" Riddle took the steep winding drive in low gear. They moved steadily higher. The white marble heads of women on small Grecian pedestals watched them pass. Further up was another gate, a swirling fan of wrought iron. Riddle had to get out of the car to unlatch it. The syncopation of chirping crickets came out of the gardens that grew in the belly of the villa's grounds. From where he stood he could see the road winding below. It was empty, but the idea that another was still behind him lingered like the patter of falling drops after a rain had stopped.

The villa was a tall white Corinthian affair with a red-clay roof and blue tile porte-cochere. Two stone dragons guarded the door. A gleeful Pan teased them from a central fountain, playing jets of water from his pipes. Candy fumbled with the lock on the two oak doors. When she got them open they led into a long marble hall. A double row of sconces with bulbs in the shapes of flames lit the corridor. They followed the light to a sunken living room. The walls were lined with gold mirrors, and stone benches with velvet cushions sat like dogs on splayed paws.

"Awful, isn't it?" Candy smirked. "And it could have been so nice. Imagine the money that's gone into it. They could have done something really tasty, instead of this ravish-me-in-Rome monstrosity. But wait until you see the bedroom," and she skipped off, dragging Riddle by the lapel of his jacket.

Upstairs the rooms were smaller. Candy ran down the hall, poking her head in doorways like a potential buyer. When she finally reached the master bedroom she swung the door open with a flourish. "You won't get anything like this at the Ritz. You see, this house"—she tossed it off with a sweep of her hand—"has been owned by a succession of lecherous impotents. You know what a lecherous impotent is? I'm an expert on the subject. It's a man who thinks about sex everywhere but in bed. That's why this bedroom had to be like something out of a Victorian porno novel . . . it was intended to keep the master's mind on the task. Personally I think it could be improved with a television. There's nothing sexier than TV. What do all those honeymooners do in their motel rooms? They watch the tube. They bang away all day to game shows. There's nothing sexier than a cheap motel and blaring TV. But we'll have to make do with this nasty-naughty boudoir." She pulled him down to the enormous four-poster bed. "Look, the sheets are real silk. Now kiss me, Jamie Riddle. Kiss me for old times' sake. Then we'll take a bath, and start all over."

Moonbeams filtered through the misted oval window of the bathroom. Riddle's eyes flickered shut, and the silver daggers of light where the spray from the moon struck the griffin's-mouth faucet dissolved into blackness. Candy had prepared his bath with bubbles and scent, and now he floated on the edge of sleep. He didn't want to sleep, not now, not without Candy beside him, but the water was as warm as heaven. It was as warm as it had been in Maxico, where Carry had made love with him in the moist sand and afterward they waded out and she saw a shark. "Look out, there's a shark," only it had been a sailfish, and he saw the ice blue fin cutting through green water. But if it had been a shark? . . . And then an impassive grey head floated in front of him, the head of a shark? No, the eyes were too clever for the eyes of a shark. They were wily, bright eyes, and then there were human features, and finally the image became the remarkable face of Radan. His eyes were intense, burning over an aquiline nose. His lips were parting in a wolfish grin, smiling and talking at the same time. Remember, Jamie? Remember what I say? Repeat it for me. Riddle obeyed, mouthing the words silently . . . "The kingdom of heaven must be won by violence, and the violent bear it away." And then the face of Radan drifted back and his hand emerged. He told Riddle to give him his hand, because only by seeing his hand could Radan tell if Jamie was ready. Riddle reached out for him . . . but Radan was no longer standing there, and it was cold where Radan had stood, and when Riddle broke the water, his leg jerked convulsively and he opened his eyes with a start.

Something had changed. The house was dead still. He had no idea how long he had been asleep in the bath. An hour at least, but something had changed. He wrapped a towel around him and stepped into the cold, dark hall. There was no light from the bedroom, but in the glow of moon that poured through the windows he could see the door ajar. "Candy?" No response. He said her name a little louder. Still nothing. In the bedroom he could make out only fuzzy shapes. More moonlight, this time a mottled pool, fell shimmering on the bed. "She's asleep," and somehow that was a relief. He let the towel fall to the floor, and rolled quietly next to her. "Candy?" He slid his hand across her shoulder. She was lying on her side, her face away from his. He ran his lips along the back of her neck. She was dripping wet. "You've come to bed without drying, darling." But there was also an odor. The water was warm and that odor was too sweet for scented water. "Candy?" Her hair was matted. The sheets were drenched. Why would she go to bed like that?

His lips had met hers, and when he finally opened his eyes he was staring into hers, and they were wide, unseeing. There was blood everywhere.

Riddle sat on the edge of the bed, his head tilted to the door, listening, trying to sharpen his vision in the darkness, gradually directing his eyes away from the faint scratches of moonlight at the window to the darker and darker places.

Moving instinctively now, he slipped off the bed, withdrew slowly to the wall. He stood still, listening again . . . to his own breath, and nothing else. As if directed by their own intelligence, his fingers now began to prance like spiders along the cold plaster wall. There was a moment after they found the light switch that they paused, uncertain, perhaps a little afraid.

Then the lights were on. Candy's neck had been slit wide open. The gaping smile was still draining blood, soaking up half the bed.

The scene held him, the throat sliced like that, the arms twisted in and out of bloody sheets. It had happened like this before, he thought. Cairo. Now this. Something was beginning. It was going to be bad, much worse than this death of Candy d'Light. It was like footsteps down a hallway, coming upstairs, heard from behind closed doors. There were no footsteps, there was only silence. But there was something to see. Turn your head, he told himself. Turn your head and you'll see that this is no ordinary murder. This is only the beginning . . . "The beginning?" He said that out loud, and the sound of his own voice frightened him. Now he no longer wanted to look but the muscles of his neck would not respond. It was too late. His eyes had already started their crawl across the room, until they were forced, finally, to see what had been written on the mirror.

The letters were smeared in lipstick, smeared in a childish scrawl. There was no sense or logic to it at all. The killer had written the words, but no one could have known. That phrase had been Riddle's secret. No one but Riddle could have known what it meant. Except the words were there, smeared in Candy's lipstick, smeared by a grinning, taunting hand . . . Someone had written on the mirror, "What right have you to butcher me, Riddle?"

And that was something no one could know, or had the right to repeat.

Chapter 7

YEARS before, Jonathan Riddle had explained to his son that abuse of the proprieties would not be tolerated. Money alone, Jamie was told, was not sufficient. The *rightness* of things was sacrosanct, not to be violated with impunity. And so when eighteen-year-old Jamie tried to save Carry after Burt had begun slapping her off the walls for drinking, Jonathan summoned the security head, Frank Ketchem, to beat Jamie senseless. Which was the final stage in Jamie's education into the strictures of the Riddle code.

It had taken him a long time properly to learn his lessons, but on that last night in Swan's Way he got them down pat. Good boys got candy, bad boys got the stick. Any fool could be taught that. The difficulty had been, how did one survive it and still maintain some bit of self-respect?

It was Carry who had come up with the answer. She found Jamie in the tea room after Ketchem had finished with him. She held a cold, moist cloth to his face. She said that she loved him very much, and when he was quiet, nearly asleep, she told him, "You've got to be strong, darling. Don't ever let them walk on you again. You can't let them get away with it even once, or they'll just keep on doing it."

All right. So, if good boys got candy, and bad boys got the stick, then the thing to do was just get the biggest stick.

Eventually, that was where Radan came in.

The year prior to the entrance of Radan had not been a good one for Jamie Riddle. He had left Swan's Way literally burning bridges. First he set fire to the recreation room where Frank Ketchem and his men spent their free time. Next he gutted his father's greenhouse, killed the Dobermans that he had always hated, and finally stole Burt's Alfa. Then, foot on the floor and hand on the horn, he took it once around the grounds and was gone.

Six weeks later he was living in Paris with an English girl named Angie. Angie had an import business, nearly authentic North African artifacts that she sold to tourists via a network of students. After a few days she took Riddle in as a partner, and he promptly eliminated the middle man (customs) and had the stuff smuggled in direct. All went smooth as silk until Angie met up with Bernard Erhart.

Riddle was never exactly sure what had happened. Erhart was a bona fide heroin dealer, but Riddle and Angie had stayed away from smack—it was too ugly. At first it seemed a joke: Erhart, the fat kraut, threatening Angie, an ex-English schoolteacher. Neither she nor Riddle took it or him seriously. Until the night Riddle came home and found her. Erhart had raped her, broken the fingers on her left hand, then beaten her unconscious. She died three days later from internal bleeding.

After that night Riddle began to drink. The business he'd shared with Angie collapsed, and he hadn't the strength to begin another. Whatever belongings he had owned were left in the apartment he had shared with Angie. After a night in the hospital with her he couldn't face going back. Eventually he returned to London, where he got a dirty cold-water flat. It was done in brown paint and looked directly onto the grey back of a cannery. The smell was horrible, and even at night the noise impossible. He had nothing to brighten the room. He bought two plastic shades to cover the bare bulbs. The rest, the clumsy wood furniture, the frayed brown carpets, he tolerated. In the day boys played against the walls outside. At night drunks congregated on the stoop, swearing and talking until dawn. Riddle hadn't the courage to silence any of it. No one knew him. He spoke to nobody. He had no money, none at all, and he badly needed a job. He spent hours combing the help-wanted ads, but it never got beyond that.

One evening, when the drunks were particularly loud, he left his room and began to walk the streets. It was somewhere in that night that he met Toby. Through Toby he met Eric, and Eric told him, "If you want a job, I can help." A week later Riddle found out what kind of work his friends did. They took him to meet Radan.

The first thing Riddle saw when he walked into Radan's hotel room in Paris was Eric standing in the corner with a butcher's knife in his hand. No one said anything. Apparently they wanted the full effect to sink in. Riddle backed toward the wall. Radan called him by name and then said, "All right, my son, I think you'd better take that knife away from your friend before he kills you." Riddle fought like a bobcat, but in the end Eric could have killed him. Still Radan was impressed enough, and after a month of intensive training the old man gave him a job. It was not the sort of job Riddle had been considering in the want ads, but it paid a good deal more. "You will be working for me, on loan as it were, to Israeli intelligence," Radan eventually told him. "You will be a mercenary, but I demand a good deal more loyalty than such a title normally implies. Understand that the Israeli government does not customarily employ mercenaries. However, I have a special arrangement with them. There are times when their own agents become too great a diplomatic liability. And so I have built up a cadre of men which I put at their disposal. I will come to know your mind, and I shall be as a father to you." Spoken in Radan's biblical cadence, which at first made Jamie smile.

He soon stopped smiling as the truly esoteric portion of his education commenced. When it was done, his ability to live up to Carry's injunction was beyond question. He possessed tremendous strength, and speed. He was not to be walked on again.

If Riddle's turning point had been with Radan and Toby and Eric in that room in Paris, it wasn't until the first run that he realized the extent of it. Obviously Radan had thought it all out, based on information he'd carefully collected. It was much too neat to be a coincidence. "There is a man who has been causing us trouble," Radan had told Riddle at the briefing. "He is a heroin dealer. His name is Bernard Erhart, and I want you to kill him."

So, big sticks were for hitting after all.

Riddle spent three weeks hunting Erhart. He finally tracked him to a villa in the Alps. The villa had one main access, a long winding drive, bordered on either side with thick hedges and high grass. Riddle waited in the grass all night. It was cold and he'd brought nothing with him but a silver-handled switchblade that Toby had given him. In the morning, numb with cold, a little faint from lack of sleep, he caught up with Erhart.

The man stepped outside. His poodle was pulling at the leash. Riddle waited until he was at the edge of the drive, then moved out and pulled him into the grass. Riddle's first slash missed the throat and caught Erhart across the eyes. The wounded man bolted deeper into the undergrowth. Riddle finally caught him again in the trees, and this time he finished the job.

Toby sat immobile in a faded maroon wing chair facing the only window in his hotel room. He had not moved since Riddle had begun to tell the story of Candy's death. He had spoken only twice. Once to ask if Riddle had removed all traces of himself before leaving the house, extinguished the lights, locked the doors and so forth. When Riddle described the body, Toby swore.

It was late afternoon. The yellow lace curtain filled with a warm breeze. Beyond the city was the steady din of traffic, broken now and again by the whine of a horn. Toby knew Riddle must be dead tired. He had looked very bad when Toby found him on the doorstep of his room at the Montmartre. Toby had plied him with coffee and given him wine, which brought back his color. For a while Riddle had even become animated, pacing about the room, smoking one cigarette after another. But now as the story was almost finished, he was clearly exhausted. He was having difficulty keeping his thoughts straight. At times he would leave sentences unfinished, or linger on trivia. He mentioned that Candy had always been afraid of cancer, and she used to say, "All of us just want to be told that everything is going to be all right. That's the big secret of life. We're all just kids, and so we all have the same secrets."

"I'm afraid I don't follow," Toby prodded gently.

Riddle turned to him with red-lined eyes. "What she meant by that?" He sat slumped against the wall. He had been letting the words dribble out to empty spaces in the room as if he were dictating to a recorder.

"No, about what happened in the woods."

"The woods?" Riddle gave him a dazed look.

"Yes, you said that it had started in the woods. I don't see the connection between Erhart's death and—"

"He must have tripped," Riddle began automatically. "Erhart I mean. He'd been running through the brush. Maybe he was blind at that point. Did I tell you I hit him in the eyes first? Yes. Well, he was running for all he was worth, for his life. Then he fell. He was on all fours. He turned to me. But all I could see was Angie's body. I went crazy. Everything that Radan had told me, everything that he had taught, it all suddenly took over. I had no control over what I was doing. I was—" He broke off.

"What, man? What were you going to say?"

"A kind of monster." Riddle said it very seriously, and looked to see if Toby was affected. He wasn't.

"The connection, Jamie. What's the point? What are you trying to get at?"

"I told you, dammit. What Erhart said."

"No, Jamie. You didn't. What did Erhart say?"

"Oh, come on, man! Listen to me. He said the same thing that was on the mirror. No one else was around. No one could have heard. Just before I cut his throat out, he yelled at me, 'What right have you to butcher me, Riddle.' Don't you *see*, Toby?" Riddle's voice that had reached a shout was now dropping to a near-whisper. "Erhart said the same words that were on the mirror."

Chapter 8

IT was dark when Riddle awoke, and for an instant he could not remember where he was. He saw Toby's suitcase on the floor but he was alone in the room. A ragged strip of wallpaper, faded and stained, hung from the ceiling like an elephant's ear. There was something wrong with Riddle's eyes. One minute the room was washed in shadows, the corners lost in murky darkness, the chairs and tables merely skeletal shapes, then suddenly everything was drenched in dull red haze. It was as if some glowing Martian cloud had seeped through the window. First blackness, then the opaque red aura. It went on like that. Finally he realized the intermittent bath of light came from a pulsating neon sign on an adjoining rooftop. For some reason it made him think of Candy. "Her body's still there." Why did he say that? To bury an even uglier thought.

Riddle lay still on the bed. He found himself counting the seconds between the blinks of neon. He had no idea when it had begun. It was just counting. "One . . . two . . . three . . ." Then he was counting footsteps. A toilet flushed. The walls seemed to shake, and someone was coming down the hall outside the door. Riddle waited for the footsteps to fade, but they just kept on coming. When did Toby say he was returning? He couldn't even remember him leaving. Must have been asleep. The footsteps stopped right outside the door. He wanted to call out, "Toby," but he couldn't. What if it wasn't Toby? Surprise was his edge. Don't waste it. And the door, the goddamn door isn't even locked. He told himself to move. Move!

Riddle was standing beside the door. He had now locked it. *"Jamie?"* A whisper from whomever it was out there. He ignored it. Just as Radan taught him. "There are going to be many people who will come to know your name, so you must judge them by the heart."

"Jamie, for godsakes, it's me. Open the door!"

Riddle was ready for anyone now, stock still against the wall. His right arm was raised high above his head. It was slightly cocked, the fingers, gently waving, loose. First it would snap at the wrist, and then that force would multiply until his hand would be like a hammer. *Jamie, what have you done with your hands?*

Suddenly it was over, because it was Toby after all, and he was nothing to attack. It was as if he had already been broken. Riddle could see that, even in the half-light of the hotel corridor. He looked pale. His features seemed soft and swollen like warm putty. His eyes were bloodshot, and for a moment Riddle had the thought that they had somehow switched places, because that was how he himself must have looked only a few hours before when he showed up on the very same spot. Perhaps Toby was more affected by the story of Candy's death than he had originally let on. Maybe that stoical reticence had only been a front. But Toby hadn't even known Candy, and anyway he wasn't one to break like that. Toby had seen too much death. . . . Riddle knew what had happened before Toby spoke his first word. Something else had surely gone wrong. Riddle had been right from the first instant lying beside Candy's dead body. Her death was no isolated murder. Something was, indeed, beginning. Now Eric was dead. Riddle simply knew it.

Riddle had started counting again, an automatic buffer to keep his mind from picturing the images too clearly. He stood before the window, a finger curled around the curtain rod, staring out across the rooftops. This time he knew when he had started counting . . . when Toby had finished telling him about Eric's death. Toby had taken the last of the wine, and his narrative had been punctuated with noisy swallows. The bottle lay at his feet. When the red neon blinked on after each six-second interval, the empty bottle caught and refracted the light like a magic talisman. "Magic." Riddle snatched the word from the idle thought and held it. "Black magic, very black magic." How else to explain it? Toby's story had been like the reenactment of some primitive ritual murder. It was brutal, if not exactly shocking because Riddle had seen it before. He knew the end of it from the start.

Toby described how he had tried to find Eric after Riddle had fallen asleep. He had called two or three numbers, and finally he found him at some girl's apartment. "It was strange because Eric told me that he'd been trying to get in touch with us. He said he had to see me, but he told me not to come where he was but to meet him in the men's room of the Ecole-Militaire Metro. He sounded damn worried. He told me there was trouble. He said there might be contracts out on all of us."

Toby went on to say how he had taken care that no one followed him to the Metro. As he continued talking, coming closer to the inevitable ending, Riddle had begun to realize what it would finally look like. He was able to visualize the empty subway station, the smells, the sounds of trains moaning from miles down the tunnels. It was almost as if Riddle had been there. He could see the door to the men's room opening. He knew what it was like to hesitate in the wake of that smell. He saw the yellow tile. When Toby finally described what he found, Riddle had been right there with him, picturing it in his mind as if recalling it from memory. He saw the arms twisted unnaturally under the body. He saw the legs spread, and the eyes glassy and wide. And the neck. Like Candy's, it had been slashed from one ear to the other. Toby's words had been coming in on him like an incantation, and even now they were still echoing. Which was why he was counting the spaces between the flashes of red light. He didn't want to hear.

"It had to be some damn maniac that did it," Toby had said. "Some fucking monster. There was blood. It was all over. There was blood on his . . . you know, down there, blood. He'd cut him down there. And then he'd written on the filthy mirror. Same words, Jamie. He'd written the same thing that you saw on that mirror with Candy."

Chapter 9

THEY would hunt the killer, just as they had hunted others in the past for Radan. This was for themselves.

They woke early, having spent a bad night of it sharing the single bed. They found a cafe near the hotel, and breakfasted on coffee and rolls. Throughout the meal Toby was indecisive. "What if we just separated? You go back to America, me to Tel Aviv. If worst comes to worst I can get Radan to draw up a three prong and clean up this mess later." But Riddle was for the hunt. He told Toby that they would begin by checking with people they knew, people who could tell them if someone had put out contracts. It was a small world, he said. Someone would talk.

At the end of the first day the two men had learned almost nothing. Toby spoke with a Belgian he had met in Spain, a freelancer now living in Paris. Toby knew the man had been out of work for some time and consequently always had his ear to the ground. At first the man was edgy. "Look, Sachs, if you want to make me an offer, then make me an offer. If not, go suck on a doorknob." Toby then got him down to the bar. They drank brandy. Toby gave him a few francs, asked about his family and finally said, "I need help with this one, Marty. I'd do it for you."

The Belgian frowned. He waited for a young man in a green beret to collect an armful of books and records and get up from the adjoining table, then said, "I think we can assume your friend, Eric Black . . . is that his name?" Toby nodded. ". . . well, I think we can assume that Black was hit by a professional. I heard that someone was taking out contracts. No names, of course. But someone was looking. I went to my man, Jean, but he couldn't get me the deal. I heard it was being handled through Henri Blocker. You know him?"

Toby pressed more money into his hand and left.

It took Riddle a day to find Henri Blocker, which as it turned out was not his real name. He was called Blocker in the trade and among the paid killers for whom he acted as a kind of recruiter, but as Henri Regnault he owned a nightclub in St. Michele.

Riddle found his way to Blocker's club on the afternoon of the third day. It had rained in the morning, and the streets were still slick, reluctant to dry in the timid sunshine. The club lay in a block of grey tenements that squatted to the curb. Laundry hung on lines between black iron fire escapes.

The entrance was down an aborted alley. The door was heavy metal, suggesting it led to a back stage. Inside it was dark. Chairs were piled to the ceiling on tables. Two women were mopping the floor and chattering to each other in Algerian. Riddle asked where the owner was, and one of them pointed to the stairs at the rear. The door at the top bore a silver lamé star. There had once been a name in the center but someone had rubbed it out. Riddle knocked and a raspy voice told him the door was open.

Henri Blocker looked neither like a man who arranged contracts, nor like a Parisian night club owner. Actually, he might have been a scholar. Not a university man necessarily, but perhaps someone found in public libraries. A man who worked merely for the love of study, Riddle thought. He wore tweeds and a tattersall shirt. The cuffs were frayed, and he had a battery of pens in the breast pocket. Thick rimless glasses made him seem especially vulnerable.

A plate of beans congealed on the desk. A small china lion stood absurdly on a riffled stack of papers. Thumbtacked to the wall were photographs of naked women, strippers who had passed through Blocker's hands at one time or another. Riddle told Blocker his name, but apparently the man already knew who he was.

"You looking for a job?"

"No."

"I can get you a job, Riddle. I can always get you a job. You got a good reputation."

"I want to know about one of your clients," Riddle told him.

"You mad at someone?"

Riddle leaned forward, resting both palms on the desk. "I want to know who hit Eric Black."

Blocker had a cigarette between his lips, a ready match. When Riddle spoke he blew it out, the cigarette still unlit. "What are you trying to be, a heavy with me, Riddle? Why don't you sit down and stop acting like an African." There was a look-you-know-how-I-work entry, two or three other phrases that skirted the issue and finally, "I can't tell you that kind of thing."

Riddle became angry. He told Blocker that the man who had arranged for Eric's hit was not a regular client. Blocker admitted that this was true. "But I can make trouble for you with your regulars. I start telling them that you've been fucking around with their areas. You know what I'm saying, Blocker? It's a small world. Can you afford to lose your reputation with the regulars? You know I know those people. What if I were to tell them that you've been fucking off. They'll believe me. Can you afford to lose a client like the syndicate?"

Blocker hesitated, weighed his alternatives. The scales settled in favor of conversation. He shrugged away his scruples.

"Yeah. I arranged a contract between three of my people and a young man." Grudging admiration tinged his voice. "You're a tough fucker, just like I heard, Riddle. But I want you to know that I didn't know that the hit was your friend Black, not until afterwards."

"What did he look like?"

Blocker whistled and shook his head. "A weird one. I only saw him once, and the room was dark. He sat in the shadows and wouldn't allow me to come too close, but what I did see was strange. He had fair hair, like yours, but it was combed up and back, like so. And he wore makeup. You know, like a woman." Blocker mimed the details as he spoke. "Lipstick, rouge, eyeliner. Very sweet little fruit. He had on a sort of flowery dressing gown. And you know, he wouldn't speak to me. He had written down on a piece of paper what he wanted. I never heard his voice. He would answer yes or no to my questions by waving a sword. You know, one of those Japanese swords. He'd wave it back and forth for yes, and up and down for no."

Riddle traced his lower lip with a finger. "Who did you give him?"

"Some Algerians, and a German. I don't know which ones he took. I didn't get a commission on it. He just gave me a flat fee for search. Good money, too. Cash, American dollars."

"Nothing else?"

"Like I said, he was a strange one. He didn't talk."

A strange one. Riddle could visualize the dry perversity of a cosmetic face. He could imagine a pale hand nodding with an ornate sword. But the overall totality of Blocker's description eluded him. And somehow this was not what he would have expected. For some reason . . . it eluded him but he quite definitely *felt* it . . . he felt as though he should have known this one, as if . . . well, as if Blocker had been describing an old acquaintance. . . .

Riddle returned to Montmartre on foot, staying close to the buildings, crossing streets quickly and pausing before turning corners. At the end of a long block he had turned and heard laughing, which perversely evoked before him the remembrance of Candy's body, and the imagining of Eric Black's. Each equally precise for him in its unwanted detail.

Chapter 10

WHAT came out in the following days was like a series of photographs. Riddle once had a friend who was a photographer. From time to time he would drop by his studio and the walls would be lined with a single thematic study. Often the pictures would be of one subject, an old man for example, taken from different angles. Each shot would reveal a special aspect of the subject, but when taken as a whole it would leave the viewer with an incomplete sense of the character. At times the effect was a little frightening, like the sudden betrayal of an old friend.

It was this impression, like a series of etchings strung together and viewed from a distance or in poor light, that Riddle was left with when the facts of three days on the hunt were compiled. Toby had discovered that apparently two Algerians and one German had arrived under contract in Paris sometime within the previous two weeks. An Englishman Riddle had spent time with in Africa claimed that he had been offered a job through a friend to hit what had been described to him as an American gangster. This in itself would have meant nothing, but the Englishman maintained he turned the job down for personal reasons. When Riddle pressed him, he told a curious story.

"I meet the bloke . . . well, I can't tell you where, but it's in a room that's totally dark. He's sitting there on a sort of couch. He's got on these pink lounging pajamas. And there's this kid, you know, like a little boy. Just a little boy, maybe ten or twelve. This kid's totally naked. I walk in and there's this queer in pink pajamas running his hands all over this kid. I'm handed a letter I can barely read on account of the bad light. But anyway it's got all the facts on it. What the pay is, everything. The letter says I can ask questions so long as they can be answered yes or no. So while I talk to this queer, he's just sitting there touching this naked kid. I couldn't believe it. I'm standing there like some jerk talking about money or something, and this queer is just shaking his head yes or no, and all the time laying his hands all over this kid. And his hands, you know it was just too weird. They were painted, you know, with nail polish. Red, too. Bright red. I couldn't see his face, but I could make out he had lipstick on. I mean it was very weird, you know?"

Next there was an unconfirmed report from a friend of Toby's in the Sureté which said that an investigation was on following the murder of a farm boy in the south of Paris. When Toby had first mentioned this, Riddle laughed. "Yeah, man, that ties right in with that item I clipped from the newspaper the other day."

"What?"

"Oh, you remember, the attack by a muskrat on a woman."

But when Toby had finished his story its pertinence became very clear, and for Jamie it was no laughing matter. The boy had been missing for several weeks when his body was found in a field not far from his home. He had been dead only a few hours. He had been mutilated, and his throat had been cut.

"By 'mutilated,' " Toby explained, "my friend meant that his genitals had been cut off, and his body had been smeared with blood. And the killer had slashed him across the eyes."

"I see," Riddle said quietly.

Gradually geography became more and more a factor. Somehow Toby discovered that not far from where the boy had been murdered, a farmer had filed a complaint against a wealthy American whom he claimed had castrated one of his bulls. Riddle thought it was pretty dicey, but Toby maintained, "We're dealing with some kind of pervert, so it could fit." Furthermore a check with realtors in the area turned up that a young American had in fact recently taken an eight-room villa overlooking the Le Mont vineyards.

And finally they got a name.

They met in a bar. It was six in the evening. The lights of the city splashed across wet pavement. Riddle was drinking a beer when Toby sat down at the table, He asked if Toby wanted one. Toby said yes, and then, "I've got a name. That villa, it was rented by an American named Swen. Does that mean anything?"

"Swen?"

"The first name is Tom."

"Tom Swen?"

"Yeah. Doesn't that mean anything to you, Jamie?"

Riddle said it didn't but he agreed to try it out on the Englishman in the morning.

Riddle met him in a park near the Gare de Lyon. The Englishman was a little drunk. As they talked they slowly circled a large pond where schoolboys sailed boats. The Englishman wore a seaman's blue pea coat. He had the collar turned up and walked with his head down as if to avoid recognition.

"You know, if I tell you these things, Jamie, where would I be? I tell you his name and where you can find this bloke, and then you go hit him. Well all right, but what if you muck it up? Then he comes looking for me, and his two Arabs." The man pronounced "Arab" like a '20's vaudeville singer ... A-rab. "I mean, where would I be then?"

"I wouldn't blow it," Riddle said seriously.

"No, I suppose you wouldn't. Not you. But just the same, it breaks the code. If we start breaking codes in this business, then where will it end? I don't care, myself. I don't give a tinker's damn what you do to the queer, but there's codes at stake here. Understand me?"

One of the boats, a slick three-master with a jolly roger standard, capsized, and its helpless captain began to cry. The two men watched as they spoke. "If I gave you a name of the area, and a possible name of the man, would you confirm it?" Riddle said.

"That'd be sort of fitting," the Englishman answered without smiling. "I'll just shake my head, the same way he did."

Then Riddle said, "Tom Swen in the Le Mont area."

And that was it.

It began as a dream. Night after night, year after year, the same dream, until the dream became an obsession. He saw himself on a dry plain, ringed by flat horizons. From one horizon to the other there was only dry cracked earth and jagged black rock. The rock stood silhouetted defiantly against a purple sky. It was from this dream that the truth emerged.

He was born with the name Tommy Swen. It was not, however, his real name. The truth was something quite different. He grew up in a land that was similar to the land he saw each night in the dream. Only the land of his home was not so dry and not as flat. Perhaps it was a good place for a boy to grow up. There were horses to ride, the dogs for company. There were cows and goats, cats and chickens. The town he lived in was small and everyone knew him. "Hello, Tommy, how are you today?" the shopkeepers would ask. "Hello, Tommy. Hello, Tommy. Hello . . ."

Tommy Swen? That wasn't his real name. Why did they call him that? He hated them for believing the lie. God, how he hated them. Why didn't they recognize the truth?

The truth being that Jamie Riddle had stolen his life. Well, not really Jamie Riddle. At least that wasn't his real name. But that wolf who called himself Jamie Riddle, mean and taking another's life just like a wolf, that one had stolen his life. And that was the real truth.

Tommy did not understand exactly how the truth had come to him from the dream. But as far back as he could remember, he had always had the dream. Then one day he realized the truth. Realized was the right word. No one had told him the truth—not his parents, not the postman, not his teacher, no one. The truth had simply come.

He thought he was about three or four when he knew the truth, but he believed that the truth had always been inside of him. After all, the dream was a kind of memory, and the memory was of a time that was before his birth.

It began like a fantasy but, unlike those fantasies that young children outgrow, this one became more real with time, as if he were slowly gaining his sight. The dream first; then he knew the truth; finally he began to hunt the wolf.

He began collecting photographs of the wolf, and stories of the wolf and the wolf's family. Whatever he could get, magazines, newspapers, anything. Not that he needed to know what the wolf looked like. Of course he knew what the wolf looked like. That was the whole point. He knew everything about the wolf. After all, it was his life that the wolf was leading. But until he was old enough to begin the hunt, the clippings helped keep the truth close to his heart.

At eighteen he began the real hunt. He followed the wolf . . . Mexico, Paris . . . He lived in cheap one-night hotels, spent whole nights in blackened doorways. He watched and he listened.

Once he lost the wolf. For a long time the wolf just disappeared, and when he finally found the wolf again he saw that he had become strong, very strong.

But terror, Swen knew, would win the victory. Terror would be his weapon against the wolf.

Knowledge of terror had been bred in the hate, and the hate was all-consuming. "Hello Tommy, how are you today?" How he hated them for that. It wasn't his name. That was the lie the wolf had perpetrated. The wolf had tricked him on that flat plain, and now he hated them all. They called him Tommy and that was proof that they were in league with the wolf. All of them—all the postmen, the teachers, the shopkeepers, all the people he saw on the streets, the ones he saw in magazines or television, or heard on the radio, they were all in league with the wolf. Even the animals, the cows and horses, dogs and cats, were in league with the wolf. And he hated them too.

But most of all he hated the wolf. In fact his hate for the wolf was so great that at times it became something else. Yes, he wanted to hurt the wolf, to break him and then finally kill him, but there were times when it was as if he almost . . . loved the wolf? No! There may have been a bond between them, a special bond, but it wasn't love. He didn't understand it, but what he felt for the wolf frightened him . . . Well, then, kill the wolf and be done with it, he told himself.

Except the wolf was so strong. And that was why he had hired his lovely boys—he especially liked the blond American who resembled him—to help him track the wolf, and now, more recently, others to begin to help him destroy the wolf and those about him . . . Cairo . . . that ridiculous tart in Paris . . . the friend in the Metro lavatory . . . a nice touch, that. His boys, of course, didn't know the truth, but they would do their part, and finally the wolf would be done away with.

Once Swen had seen the wolf at the fullness of his strength, his violence, and it was frightening, but then the wolf had smothered that strength because he was afraid of it himself. And although he was certain that strength was not dead, he was also convinced it would not fully awaken again inside the wolf unless he too knew the truth. And he would see to it that the wolf would die before he knew the truth.

Yes, the impostor who had robbed him of his life, who presumed to call himself Riddle, would die. And soon. . . .

Chapter 11

RIDDLE had become too intense with it. Toby had awakened in the night to hear him pacing the floor, padding to the window, a lean shadow hovering on the wall in the persistent neon. Once when Riddle had been rummaging through a leather shoulder bag for cigarettes Toby had even caught snatches of his private whisperings, soon replaced by the smoke sucked deeply into his lungs.

By the early morning Riddle was asleep, stretched out on the edge of the bed. Toby didn't wake him. He rose alone, trembling in the skin of cold air, and stood on one leg to draw up his trousers. When he was ready, his pockets stuffed with francs, his hand on the knob of the door, he paused, or perhaps was held for a second by Jamie's vulnerable posture. You certainly wouldn't know how he hunts, to see him there now. Sleep, the leveler, Toby thought, as he slipped out the door.

Riddle was up when Toby returned. He was sitting at the desk, scowling at the yellowed map that was thumbtacked to the plaster. The edges of that map had curled past the tacks, and the stems still threw the shadows of the early sun on the wall. The map revealed where they were going. Toby had prepared the route with lines of red ink, and now he had sandwiches, a bottle of burgundy, and a thermos of coffee.

"But you got the guns, didn't you?" Riddle's savagery was also innocent, which was part of his key.

"Yeah, I got the guns."

"Let's have a look."

Toby drew them out of his shoulder bag, two ugly bundles of crumpled oil cloth. "I don't think you've seen anything like these before, Jamie. They're only .22's but they're fully automatic."

Riddle sighted down the barrel into the spray of light coming through the blinds. The weapon was not much larger than a .45 and no heavier at all. It had an unfinished aluminum grip with a long pencil barrel. The magazine, like a box of kitchen matches, sat below the barrel. "It fires both auto and fully auto. I've packed ten clips each."

"This is good."

"I've had the bullets dum-dummed."

"Yeah?"

"And these things are expensive, a bitch to come by, so don't louse them up."

"Well, I'll try not to."

"They're an edge, Jamie, they'll give us an edge." . . .

But an edge against what? They had driven into the heart of the countryside. The narrow pot-marked road cut like a snake through the head-high grass. It was hot. Great coruscations where the sun flared off dry foliage obliterated whole sections of the landscape with impossible glare. It was dead still. The leaves of an occasional poplar tree were frozen, glittering in the heat like tiny squares of scarecrow tin. Even the high drone of insects had stopped.

Earlier in the day Toby had said, "We'll find this guy. If he wants a war, we'll bring it right to his doorstep." Only now the elements froze him, riveted him to the wheel of the Volkswagen.

They had stopped by the side of the road. There was the popping and clicking of the slowly cooling engine. There was the heat and static bursts of shimmering light. Toby's sweating hands were kneading the greasy plastic. "It's weird, man. There's something weird."
And Riddle nodded because he too had felt uneasy. "It's the hour of the noonday devil."
"The *what*?"
"The hour of the noonday devil. Between noon and vespers they believe that evil walks—"
"Who believes?"
"Peasants, the peasants in Greece, maybe some other places too."
"Yeah, what do they say about it?"
"Just that evil walks, wanders over the scrub brush hills."
"Well, whatever the hell it is, man, it's making me feel damn strange."
Yes, "strange," but then Riddle believed he understood these things. His life had been wrapped, smothered in the dead still minutes of the noonday devil before. Once, years ago, there had been a day like this, the day he'd known he'd lost his father. He had been standing in the garden behind Swan's Way. There had been birds singing, flies buzzing, a breath of wind. Then there was nothing. Everything stopped, and he *knew* his father was gone. No one else knew it because there was a man who looked like his father, spoke like him, but at four years old Jamie knew that it wasn't really *his* father. Maybe it was someone else's. But his father had been killed by the lion or whatever it had been, far away in Africa. This man was too mean to be *his* father.
He had once told Radan about that day in the garden when he had stood behind the gates of Swan's Way. "Ah, the hour of the noonday devil. And were you aware that evil was walking?"
"Well, let's just say I felt something. . . ."
"Then remember how it was, Jamie Riddle. For real evil is not the absence of good, but the mirror image of it. It will not be conquered with charity. It must be put to the stake, and you can recognize it at the hour of the noonday devil."
All right. Maybe Radan was crazy, maybe not. But now they

had come to pound the stake into a man named Tommy Swen. Only now they were fixed on the hot vinyl seats under the baking tin roof, surrounded by the quiet spikes of grass. And Riddle felt very close to the madness that had sometimes been Radan, what with all his talk of evil, abstract and absolute.

"Up there's the house," Toby said. It was some half-a-mile beyond the road, perched in a ring of bright ivy and tall trees.

They separated. Toby would take the front and Riddle the back. That first half-mile was a low crouching walk through the high yellow grass. They might have been two small animals, mice or rabbits. Their world was constricted to brown earth and dry grass, and when the wind came up it bent the grass like swells through deep water.

Toby paused when he reached the wall, then a quick peek through the folds of ivy, and he went over. He was in a red brick courtyard. Once a garden had floated in the oval beds between the walks; now there were only weeds. Where there was once a proud Spanish façade, now the white stucco was greying and chipped. Blue shutters hung from rusty hasps at sad angles. The once regular imbrication of red clay tiles was badly shaken. Me too, Toby thought, recognizing his fear.

And as always he met fear head on with anger. Met it, didn't defeat it, and he was beginning to worry about it as he caught his breath in the splay of the front door.

He had forgotten about the fear, but then he had not been on a hunt for a long time. He'd been hunted, yes. He and Jamie had been hunted like animals in Cairo, and before that he'd made a sprint across Lebanon with every Moslem cutthroat east of Mecca on his tail. As the hunted he could run and feint, show the colors and then slip out the side door. Conflict wasn't inevitable. The object was to avoid confrontation. As the hunter, it was the key. You went looking for it, it was the whole point. The hunt: a chase until the kill. The hunt was Jamie's world, not his. After all, Radan had bred Jamie for it. Jamie was his special creation . . . his hand-made monster. At least that was what everyone said. Radan would never admit that, but Toby had seen Jamie hunt before, and it was true. Which was why he thought Radan had been full of crap when he told Riddle he hadn't gone far enough down the road. Riddle on the hunt was pretty far down anyone's road.

At one point Toby wondered if he shouldn't just wait at the door until Jamie entered from the rear. After all, the hunt was really Jamie's meat. Toby could just sort of keep an eye out, just wait where he was and then . . . oh, hell, that was chicken shit. His fear wasn't that bad.

It was worse. He had tried the door and it wasn't even locked. It was as if somebody wanted him to step inside. He was in an umbrageous green tiled hall, there was trash against the wall and no furniture, like an entrance to a filthy hospital where poor Catholic girls went for abortions . . . it smelled of urine and dry rot, and as he took the blow from the rifle butt he absorbed all these impressions as if it were going to be his last moment alive and all this was all he was ever going to see of life so he might as well make the best of it. His head exploded and he went down with one last thought: if I was the one who was being hunted they wouldn't have got me either. . . .

He was in a room. They had carried him there. Dragged him actually, and his shins hurt because he hadn't been able to make the stairs, and when they pulled him up his shins had bounced off the steps. He hadn't opened his eyes because maybe they would think he was unconscious and not hurt him anymore. But even without looking he knew the floor was tiled like the hall had been. There was dirt all over; he could feel the dust on his lips where he lay on the tiles. And he knew there were two of them—that was obvious from the way he had been dragged. His greatest triumph was to realize that at least one of them was French. Garlic, he could smell garlic on the man's breath. Italians also ate a lot of garlic, but somehow the French had a slightly different odor. Jamie had said that the target had hired two Arabs, but at least one of these men was French. He'd bet on it. He already had.

So he was lying on the floor of a dirty tiled room. There were two men, one of them French, perhaps both. At least he wouldn't die in ignorance. Beautiful, at least I can say where and by whom I was killed.

A third man walked in. Lighter footsteps than the others.

Toby felt his head jerked up by the hair, then a voice in English: "That's not the right one," and his head was dropped back to the floor. For an instant he actually thought he might survive. They were after Jamie, they might leave him be. He could stay where he was on the floor, eyes closed, unmoving. Later there might even be an opportunity for escape, or even to take them, but for the moment he figured he was safe. Something slammed into his left side, just below the ribs, and what came through the pain was that this third man wasn't French, that he was the American who'd spoken English ... no doubt the target, the one that had killed Eric and Jamie's girlfriend, and now he was going to kill him.

At one point when the blows came jackhammering one after another Toby opened his eyes and saw that the American had left the room and it was the other two that were going to smash up his kidneys, pop his bladder, little by little, kick by kick. They were standing over him like hockey players, laying in with their boots and rifle butts, and it was getting to be a rotten way to die. And then a boot stomped his face into the tiles and he couldn't think anymore.

But he heard the shots, distant cracks of automatic fire from Jamie's pistol. The two men stopped beating him and ran to the window. One eye was closing, and bits of broken teeth were flaked on his lips. But now he was going to get back at them. Or at least Jamie was, because once Riddle caught the scent there was no escape. He was Radan's monster.

Radan had taken time perfecting Jamie. He had given him a gun, a little 9mm automatic. No bullets, just the gun. For months Riddle was never without it. He'd had to eat with it, sleep with it, carry it in his hands wherever he went. He did the same thing with knives, and when it came time to fire the gun or throw the knives, Radan told him, "Just do it. Don't think about hitting anything, just do it." Riddle made jokes about Radan's methods. He called the old man's technique "the transcendental school of bullshit." But it worked. Oh yes, it worked ... so well that Toby could understand why Riddle said sometimes he was scared of what he'd become. "Some guy could come up behind me and ask for a light and I'm afraid I'd turn around and take his head off," Riddle had once said.

"But that's good," Toby whispered, "that's good, Jamie. Don't try to control it now. Just let old Radan's monster take over. Don't be afraid of it now, the monster is inside you. For God's sake . . . *mine* . . . don't be afraid to let it loose." Toby said that last very softly, so that no one would hear, and he said it in Hebrew.

There was a knock at the door. One of the men at the window jumped up and ran to open it. Who else would knock? Only one of their own. The man opened the door. It was just open a crack, but Riddle's hand snaked in, three fingers like a claw, and they crushed the man's windpipe so that he wouldn't scream, and then snapped the neck like a twig. As the man began to collapse Riddle rode him into the room, a shadow on the dying man's back. He stepped in right behind him so that when the second man turned around there was an instant when all he saw was his friend stumbling back from the door, which was when Riddle fired from the hip.

Chapter 12

THE body of the man Toby insisted had been their target lay in the courtyard below. Riddle had climbed in through the rear window, met him in the upstairs hall and fired a single burst. The man was hit in the face, and the force had sent him crashing over the balcony. Now it was impossible to determine what he had looked like. Still, his hair had been blond, and Toby recalled he'd heard him speaking with an American accent. "I'm telling you, Jamie, this one is your man. He's the one," and then Toby padded back inside, leaving Riddle standing over the body.

But Radan's hour of the noonday devil was like a vacuum. The air became charged with a dry, electric stillness, and Riddle wasn't sure he didn't still sense, feel the threat. It was like a ringing in his ears, at a moment of dead silence. And he was right, because it was only the body of Tom Swen's favorite boy.

Toby found a bathroom and sat on the tiles under a shower

of cold water. Riddle poked his head in and asked, "How are you doing, man?"

"Toss me a smoke." Toby smiled. "I'm dying." The first went soggy, and Riddle left him another cigarette on the wash basin. Toby became cold after twenty minutes, and with the cold he began to feel silly. He wasn't really hurt. Bruised maybe, two teeth were chipped, tomorrow he would be sore as hell but essentially he was fit. "Fit." He played with the word a few times, sputtering it off his lips as the water ran down. Then he rose and shut the shower off. There was only one towel, a filthy one hung over the shower rod like a rag. "Pick up every disease known to man," he muttered, and tearing the curtain off a window used that instead.

Still wet, shirt clinging to his back, Toby moved down the hallway. Some of the rooms showed evidence of life, but it had been a mean, scanty life. Cots and an unmade bed with dirty sheets. A few bits of clothing strewn about. The single touch of domesticity was a pyramid of empty beer cans stacked on a window sill. It might have been a flophouse for refugees or young runaways. All the drawers had been rifled. Toby assumed Riddle had been through them because a few rooms down he was still at it. Things were being thrown to the floor. He heard the shattering of glass or porcelain. He called Riddle's name. No reply. "Jamie?"

"Come here, man. I'm here," Riddle returned, and Toby followed the voice to a door at the end of the corridor. Here the windows had been blacked out with newspapers. Riddle stood in the doorway against a curtain of darkness. His hands were on his hips and the trench coat flared out like a skirt. The expression on his face was like a bewildered matador. He seemed to be waiting for Toby's reaction to something. Toby stepped behind him into the room. Riddle pointed to the walls. "Photos?" Toby said, observing the photographs and magazine cutouts plastered all over the walls and ceilings. Riddle struck a match and Toby followed the light like a moth.

"Christ! They're all of *you*, Jamie. Every damn one is a picture of you." Riddle moved the match across the walls in a slow tour like an archaeologist illuminating the drawings in a cave.

Toby, a dumbstruck acolyte, kept chanting, "Holy shit, holy shit," and finally, "when were these taken?"

"The magazine ones are from years ago. Ten, maybe fifteen. But the photos were taken when I first came to Europe. This one is the flat I lived in in London. It wasn't long before I met you. Look at that, that one over there. They seemed to have all been taken in about a two or three week period. See the way my hair is. The guy must have followed me around for nearly a month."

"And you've no idea who he was?"

Yes, Riddle was about to say, he had no idea who the man was, but suddenly he knew that wasn't the whole truth. The whole truth was more than that. It was breaking in on him now like a dawn against a desert's purple sky, and somehow that surprising, extravagant image seemed altogether right and appropriate. The truth was . . . he merely *knew* it . . . his portrait collector had been with him all his life. He may never have realized it until now, but he also felt as though the knowledge had always been there . . . inside him. It wouldn't, couldn't, have been something that he had learned . . . more like something he had been born with.

They bought a bottle of white wine in a cafe outside Paris and then climbed to the roof of the Montmartre to finish it off. They watched the lights of the city blinking under low black clouds and talked until dawn. Toby said he would be able to join Riddle in the States after a few months. "You go to your place, see. Get the family jewels. I know a place in New York, Sixth Avenue and 47th Street. We take the stuff down there and peddle it. Strictly cash, no questions asked. Then we go to Colorado. See, I know this chick in Colorado . . . you ever been there? It's just great. You just have to sit around in the clean air. Everyone is sitting around. They're drinking beer, singing John Denver songs. All the ass you want. I'm telling you, Jamie, you got to have someone like me to show you how to enjoy yourself. Guys with a lot of bread don't know how to really enjoy it. But with me . . . I'm telling you, Jamie, this is what you've been waiting for."

At which point Riddle realized he had been waiting for something else. This may have been the first time he had been able to envision it, but he felt he had always been waiting for it. He was almost certain now. It had been that man he had killed. Toby's target. Tommy Swen was the only name they had, but now Riddle could imagine the face of this Tommy Swen. There was no real recognition, yet he could see the expression it would have had. There would have been a curled upper lip, the nostrils slightly flared, and the eyes, they would have been worst of all. Those eyes would have been the same kind of eyes he had seen in his father, or rather the man who called himself his father—vacant, predatory, disembodied like the eyes of a child's doll. Then came the thought: "I knew him." There was no real memory, no time or place, only that face and the thought: I knew him. And not just knew him once, but had always known him. It was as if he had always had that face behind him, out "there." They might have been running after one another all their lives, he and the one called Swen. At times they might have grown close, close enough to touch, while at others, they would have appeared to one another as only the merest flicker of color rounding the corners in a maze of dark streets. But the potential for mutual recognition had always been in them. For a moment the fantasy was consuming, an obsessive dream, and before it passed he said quietly but audibly, "But we've been waiting for each other all our lives . . ." He hadn't meant Toby to hear it. Hadn't been aware of Toby when he said it.

"Waiting for who, man?"

When Riddle didn't answer Toby didn't ask again. Maybe it was that girl, he figured. The only one Jamie had ever really seemed to care for. The one back home. Toby remembered her name was Carry.

Chapter 13

THERE were times in the lives of those at Swan's Way when the house itself seemed greater than its masters. So much older time was drenched into the pores of the bricks one was often lost in the still eternity of the colonnade, and to brush past those drapes, twenty feet from ceiling to floor, to watch them shiver and then return to their own stiff form, was frightening. Somehow they rang with the reflection of one's own grim mortality.

Michael Riddle was too young to understand the disquietude that lingered in the corridors of Swan's Way. He knew only that Uncle Jonathan was dead, and so he was to keep quiet and out of sight when he moved about the house, and spend most of his time outdoors.

Which was fine with Michael. He hated the house. Everything in its place, don't touch, and if you scratched the wood or the marble tops the maids scowled.

Michael was ten, and already champion of the lawns and forest. He was captain of his merciful bandit brigade that camped in the hills and gardens. He was out in full colors, a shabby green coat, a red bandanna knotted about the throat and a broad-brimmed safari hat with one side pinned up in a rakish piratical curl. In his back pocket he carried a wicked penknife with three cutting blades, and over his shoulder hung the Daisy B.B. rifle that took all his strength to cock. His patrol had been stormed all morning. There had been snipers at every turn, every field had been mined, every bush booby-trapped. He had lost three men at the creek, another to a lucky shot and he himself had been wounded in the arm. But now he had the chance to turn the tables. He went down on one knee for the near-impossible shot. Miss, and they'd be on him like a pack of wolves. Then, just as he had read in the Daisy manual, hold your breath, begin counting and squeeze.

"You're a little high," came a voice from behind him.

Michael swung around. "Who are you?"

A sly smile. "I used to be the leader around here."

The boy ran his eyes over the intruder. He certainly looked as if he had once been captain, or at any rate a bandit of importance. Even now he had that roguish mark of an outlaw. He wore a full-length military coat and a pair of extraordinary purple trousers that had seen too many campaigns. His T-shirt advertised those brutal-smelling cigarettes that Uncle Max sometimes smoked, and at his waist was the most fiendish belt buckle Michael had ever seen. It showed a snake, a cobra, Michael guessed, against a red background. The snake was coiled and grinning and ready to strike.

"I wouldn't have missed if you hadn't talked," Michael said.

"Come on, now. I didn't say a word until you fired."

There was no fooling him. "All right, you try it." He handed the intruder his rifle and watched silently as the man poured six rounds in dead center, faster than he had ever believed a Daisy could fire.

"The trick is to keep both eyes open. Don't look at the sight, look beyond to the target." Michael tried but had no luck. "You've got to keep at it. If everyone could do it, then none of us would be safe."

The intruder was slouching against the trunk of a tree. Michael noticed that his shoes, or boots really, were also made of snakeskin. Probably cobra too. "So what's your name then?" the intruder asked. "Are you a Riddle?"

"Uh huh. Michael Jamie Riddle. But I wasn't named after *the* Jamie Riddle."

"Which one is that?"

"Uncle Jonathan's son. We'd be cousins, but he ran off and became a pirate."

"Is that what they're saying these days?"

"Well, I heard that from Uncle Max. No one else talks about him very much. Uncle Max says they're scared of him. He says they're scared because he tried to burn down all the houses before he ran away." Michael stopped and looked up at the sky. "I was just a baby then, and I wasn't even living here 'cause it wasn't the summer, but Uncle Max told me they are afraid of him for that, and because he's a pirate. I don't know if it's really true. You see, Uncle Max . . . well, it's not exactly lying, but you know, he kind of exaggerates things. So I'm not sure if it's really true. About him being a pirate, I mean . . ."

The intruder had been taking out a cigarette from a silver case. He had not looked up at Michael. He had returned his cigarette case, packed down the one he had selected, and finally flipped it into the corner of his mouth and lit it. Now the intruder was looking straight at him. "I'll tell you something, Michael"—his smile was chilly—"that story about him being a pirate, it's true."

Carry leaned against the edge of the high grey marble table and pressed her fingers on the stone so her knuckles whitened. On the mantelpiece was a photograph of Jamie.

There was still some hope. She turned from where she leaned and slowly rolled herself over a white pine armrest and fell into the green brocaded sofa of eiderdown. Of course, there had been hope before, and the hope had usually come to nothing. The times she had seen Jamie since he had run off he always told her, "I'll come back to you soon." But then he would leave and "soon" was always one day, and one day never seemed to come.

She had been living on hope ever since the telegram had arrived.

A cavalier note: "WILL RETURN STOP DELAYED IN PARIS STOP J. RIDDLE STOP"

That was three weeks ago, and every day the hope had grown a little older, and soon it would fall into the ditch where all the other memories of hope languished. Carry could be tough, flip, but whenever someone mentioned Jamie, hope beat its wings.

Moving through the house, she drifted past beechwood cabinets with holly inlay, Dutch glass and gleaming cases of porcelain. In a green hall tall cream shutters were folded back. Wind rattled in the trees as she stepped outside and wandered down to the tea room in the garden.

Others had left weeks ago. First cousins and second cousins, friends of the family and the families of friends, they had all left. There was still Aunt Stella, her daughter, Sylvia, with Sylvia's husband, Joel, and their two children. There was still Max, the staff and one or two others that Carry didn't know, but for the most part they had all gone.

Carry's parents, Burt and Eleanor, had told her to leave. They said there was nothing for her at Swan's Way, that she wasn't welcome, although Aunt Stella insisted she was. Then they left too. And as Eleanor had stepped into the long black Dorchester, she turned to Carry and said, "He's not coming back. Why the hell don't you get on with your own life?"

But Jamie had come back. He had flown in to Boston, and then taken a cab to the edge of Swan's Way. He had one battered suitcase, and when he reached a secluded section of the grounds he threw his luggage over the fence and climbed over. This was entering on his own terms—an outsider. Later Carry would ask him why he had avoided the main gate, scaled the walls and tramped around in the forest with Michael for over an hour, and all he said was, "Well, I guess I felt more at home with the kid."

Carry now sat on the steps of the tea room. Puffs of breeze played with the leaves, tossing the shadows back and forth on the flagstone walk. She brushed a spray of blond hair from her eyes. Somewhere beyond the walk Jose, a pick-and-shovel gardener, was breaking soft earth and whistling to himself. Occasionally he'd pick up the words to the tune of a Beatle hit that he sang in Spanish. Carry dropped her head into the fold of her arms.

When Riddle appeared it was, quite literally, as if he had stepped out of a dream. There was the brush of leaves in the wind. There was the gardener's song. There was a clap of a boot on the flagstone walk. On the one hand, all these sounds had a reasonable place in the moment, but Carry sensed something else. She raised her head, and there were Jamie's cobra-skin boots clapping on the stones. His face was glowing like a jack-o-lantern, eyes alight with mischief. "Hello, it's me." Hello, Lazarus, back from the dead.

"Oh God!" she said, and then Jamie picked her up and waltzed her across the lawns.

Chapter 14

FOR most of them at Swan's Way Jamie Riddle's return was a most nervous event. A downstairs maid likened it to the return of Frankenstein's monster, but really it was not so much more than something like a student's jitters on the first day of class. One waited to see if the teacher was, in fact, the beast of rumor.

Aunt Stella called her guests into the drawing room. There were more than half-a-dozen of them. There were Waters and Wright, who had been Jonathan's financial advisors, Sylvia and Joel and their two children, Stella's secretary, Francis, and of course Max. Carry remained upstairs with Jamie. Nervous glances darted about the room like fireflies. Aunt Stella picked at the lips of a lion's mask on the arm of her Regency high-back chair. She thought she had told the others to sit, but for the first time no one seemed to be paying any attention to her. A crystal decanter of blood-red sherry had been laid out, but only Max was drinking.

He stood at the Indian card table, filling his glass with rattling inaccuracy. In his white cotton suit that bagged in the seat and swelled in the arms, he looked like a British colonizer gone to seed. There was a widening dark stain on his white suede loafers.

When the double doors to the drawing room opened, the voices stopped. First there was only Soames. He spoke barely above a whisper, hardly fitting to announce the passing of the Riddle crown. The long case clock where cherubs peeked from a forest of satinwood turnings began to toll. Someone said it was off, the old clock was wrong. Max, in reflex, glanced at his wristwatch, and then Jamie was standing in the doorway.

For Max those first impressions were to be measured on a private scale, just as his own life had been lived for the past twenty years by a private code. First he saw that there was indeed strength. The boy had matured. A man's voice called out "Jamie"—and Riddle let it fall like a low bid to the Oriental rug. Max approved of this. Stella raised a doughy hand to be kissed or held; Riddle ignored this too. He paced across the floor like a dancer, in near slow motion, eyes surveying the faces of the assembled, and to Max they were extraordinary eyes, not easily confrontable, intensely alive.

Max watched him light a cigarette. Stella was speaking and Riddle leaned against the door jamb. He nodded slowly to something she said. His eyes were fixed on his fingers as they took a cigarette from his case. He was smiling now, Max noted, a wintry smile. His head dipped a bit to the left. There was control, and there was strength. Good, he would need them. If there had once been something of the rebel, then now it was tempered with experience. If there was a touch of vulgarity, at the same time there was a shadow of something else, something vaguely feminine, perhaps a sign of sensitivity. Well, he would need that too.

Max had moved to the window. A blue velvet drape was tied with a black satin sash. The evening was falling from the sky. Trees cast tall shadows on the lawn, and beyond was the forest, growing dark.

Max was finished with doubt. Psychology, psychiatry, no use

for them. Throw them out. Years ago he might have worried about himself. No more. He once told himself that he was like a missionary who had gone to the jungle and traded his faith for superstition. Well, it had happened in the jungle, all right, but it was no superstition. It was real. That was why it was so important that Jamie be both sensitive and strong. He must be as sensitive as radar. If it moved into the forest like it had done with his father, then he needed to be able to sense it. He needed to be able to feel its presence. He could not wait until it wrote, or telephoned, or came banging through his bedroom door in the middle of the night. He had to realize all this from the start, know it intuitively. Because it was not something that Max could tell him about, not straight off anyway. One had to believe before one could act. Only, that was the catch. It wasn't like voodoo. The thing killed whether one believed in it or not.

Chapter 15

STELLA'S white hair was spun up like cotton candy. A tartan comforter was folded across her knees, a shawl with embroidered roses like splotches of blood draped her shoulders. She was alone with Riddle. She had contrived this moment. Dinner had passed and the guests had adjourned. She had spirited Riddle away from Carry, and had him delivered by Soames to her bedroom. Jamie went along, paying homage to the matriarch of a fallen power.

He sat on the Queen Anne, Stella on Hepplewhite. Her back was to the vanity table so that the mirror threw an image to him of her shawl that was like the wings of a rare night moth from the Amazon.

When Riddle had been sixteen Stella had caught him smoking and said, "Just where do you think you are, young man?"

Riddle had stolen a line from Eliot and said, " 'I think we are in rat's alley where the dead men lost their bones.' " Perhaps she had been a little frightened of him ever since.

"I'd welcome you to Swan's Way," Stella opened, "but one can hardly welcome one to one's own house."

"I've been told the house is mine," Riddle answered.

"Your father believed in primogeniture. Most of what you see around you, Jamie, is yours. That makes a great deal of difference."

"To you, Aunt Stella?"

"To *all* of us. Uneasy lies the head that wears the crown. You have a responsibility to the family."

"I have a responsibility to more than the family."

"Of course you do. So did your father."

"Responsibility meant something different to him than it does to me. To him it was control."

"And to you?"

"I'm not sure yet . . ." and then remembering a line of Radan's, he added, " 'perhaps the willingness to care.' "

Her face became a mask. "You're still bitter, I see."

"I haven't come back for vengeance, if that's what you mean."

"Did you come back for Carry?"

"That's part of it. I guess a big part of it."

"I understand you have been sleeping with her. I mean, you intend to. Her things have been moved into your room."

"Only for convenience."

"Don't be impertinent with me, Jamie."

"I can afford it now, aunty."

"You don't like us very much, do you?"

"You haven't made it particularly easy for me to."

"I can't see how you can say that?"

"My father tried to ruin me. Where were you, aunty? Where was anybody?"

"If your father didn't love you, he wouldn't have left you all this," she said sharply.

"An oversight."

"I don't understand."

"He never changed the will. It was drawn up when I was born. Then . . ." He was about to mention Africa, what had happened there, the change he'd felt in his father, but she wouldn't have understood that either. ". . . then he just never found anybody else . . ."

"Of course not. You were his only child. I know he would have been proud that you've come back, and proud that you've grown up."

Candy's words skimmed along the surface of Riddle's thoughts. We are all merely oversized children, she had said. "We'll see how much I've grown up. Beginning tomorrow."

"You go to Boston with Mr. Waters and Mr. Wright?" This had a cheerful inflection to it.

"Uh huh."

"That's exciting for you."

Riddle smiled now, because she was no longer playing, advancing and retreating, trying to draw him out to discover his intention. "I'll meet the broker. Steven Ganns."

"And you haven't a thing to wear."

"I'll manage."

"Oh, Jamie"—her relief oozed out—"I so wish your father could see you as you are now . . ."

Riddle had leaned forward on one arm, head turned slightly to the side. "Oh, he'll see me all right. He's waiting for me, just as I'd be waiting for him if I had died first." He paused, with a finger pointing to the floor. "Waiting down there." An easy flourish, he realized. Also dead serious.

Chapter 16

IT had been in the most unlikely corner of the world that Jamie had discovered his great-grandfather's oblique legacy. Radan had sent him to the Ivory Coast to fish for an African megalomaniac who was worshipped in the jungle as the savior of his people. The run aborted prematurely when the target was privileged to an impromptu display of Russian might. The African leader, who strutted around his cold water palace in top hat, tails and a chest full of medals that included a lion's paw and the teeth of a mongoose, became a card-carrying Communist overnight. Consequently the moment Riddle set foot in the country he was slapped into jail. Riddle's cellmates were only bits and pieces of men.

The jailer was a garish savage who affected the manners of a British solicitor and looked like an extra from a Tarzan film. "First we shall have a quiet little chat," he told Riddle. "Would you care for some tea?" Riddle nodded. One of the guards turned for the door. The other glanced at the window, and that was the instant Riddle moved. He went for the guards first. They went down like golliwogs. One had a broken neck, the other a broken back. The jailer, however, was quicker than Riddle imagined. He moved with the deceptive speed that some fat men can manage, and he had a pistol drawn and nearly aimed before Riddle caught him in the wrist with his right foot, and then followed through with an elbow to the temple.

And then he saw the pistol, a beautiful piece, hand-tooled with ivory grips. Along the barrel the artist had worked in hunting scenes of the African veldt. Sweeping down the breech was a black Jesus strolling across the surface of the Nile. Weeping crocodiles embellished the edges of the ivory grip, ending in a flourish of reeds and water lilies that circled the central trademark. It was a Westermark .38.

Westermark had been founded, maintained and was still held by the Riddles of Massachusetts.

The Riddle fortune was hatched neither from great ingenuity nor great invention. Joseph Riddle simple bulldozed certain key portions of the country's armament efforts into his pocket and built from there. From weapons it was a song and dance to domestic explosives, then a hop, skip and jump to chemicals. But if one was going to shoot them, blow them up and poison them, the least one could do was try to heal them, or if that was impossible, then ease their pain while they died. Hence: medical supplies.

Over the years the money had spread out, "like venereal disease," Carry once remarked. It was placed across the boards of family trusts, public corporations, property, stocks, bonds. The empire was generally overseen by Jonathan's financial advisors, Waters and Wright, Attorneys at Law. It was these two who now were to lead Jonathan's son, Jamie, through the rites of passage, hand him the crown and scepter, give him papers to sign and take him to Boston, where he would meet the brokers who handled the family portfolio.

They left early on the second day of Riddle's return. Carry

saw them to the limousine. She was barefoot and naked under a floor-length fur. She stood clutching it tightly against an early morning chill as Waters and Wright and finally Jamie stepped into the back of the glossy Rolls. Before the car pulled away she tapped the window. Jamie rolled it down, and while Waters and Wright looked away in silent embarrassment she kissed her lover full on the mouth.

They were an awkward party. Riddle, who had not had time to begin building even the most basic wardrobe, wore a brown corduroy suit. It was well cut, and had recently been cleaned and mended, but still it was only corduroy, and made him look vaguely like a college boy. The tie, in fact, had been from Princeton. He had found it hanging in his closet. He had no idea how it got there. Riddle had forgotten to remove the thin, silver bangle from his wrist.

Waters and Wright, on the other hand, wore Brooks Brothers. Their ties were rich and modest, and asserted with simple gold pins. Each carried a dark leather briefcase.

Waters did all the talking. He began when the car turned down the drive, and the waving, smiling figure of Carry, like a beautiful ghost of the morning, vanished over the rise. Riddle noted that he referred to money as "a figure," or "capital," or "interest." From time to time Wright would be called upon to supply a specific, usually a name or a particular figure. Once or twice he corrected Waters. "There was no buy-sell arrangement for any of the immediate family holdings prior to your father's death. However, we can assume that at least twenty-five percent . . ." Waters was saying, and Wright added on another two percent. Waters never seemed to mind Wright's interjections. His partner had a mind like a digital computer, and Waters used it as such; punch in a problem, pull out data. It was a symbiotic relationship. One got the feeling that they had been meant for each other, like Romeo and Juliet, or sharks and pilotfish. Riddle could not help seeing them as a single entity. Waterwright, he thought.

Except for the occasional request for clarification, Riddle did nothing more than listen. He sat very straight in the seat, his hands folded on his lap. Once they passed two boys walking along the road. The boys waved and only Riddle seemed to notice.

Waters had a way of jumping topics without any formal transition. Riddle found this confusing, but still managed to keep abreast. He had told himself to play it straight, learn; because it might one day be important. He once sat through Radan's more literal briefings with the same attitude.

In Boston they went directly to the brokers, who held the top two floors of a large brownstone in the center of town. Riddle was introduced to the man he was told handled the family portfolio. This was Anderson, a thin pale man with a full head of sandy hair. Had Riddle not been told by Waters as the elevator had taken them to the top floor that Anderson was *the* Anderson of Anderson, Bartlett, Capers and Hall, Riddle would have taken him for an aging clerk. He wore thick rimless glasses and looked out of place in his own office. One wall supported a bookcase by William Adam from Stoke-on-Trent and was filled with leather-bound translations of the Romans that no one had ever read, giving the place a certain degree of musty authority.

Secretaries served coffee in small white cups. There was both brown and white sugar, cream and milk.

Riddle was told that most transactions involving family holdings, "both primary and secondary," added Wright, would be handled by Mr. Anderson.

"Steven and I have worked closely for years," Anderson said. That was Steven Ganns, the functional head of most Riddle enterprises. They were to meet with him later in the day, lunch at Locke-Ober's. Riddle was not sure who was expected to pick up the check. He remembered that he and Angie used to walk checks regularly when they were broke in London.

"You will of course be able to take whatever hand in the trading you like," Anderson was saying. He pointed with a sugar spoon to a battery of telephones. Riddle had been taught that pointing with eating utensils was rude. A few grains of sugar went splattering across the desk. "When you get your feet wet, the decisions will come easily. Some points may seem complex now, but when you get your feet wet, you'll see how we run it."

Anderson was speaking to Riddle as if he were asking for a job. It wasn't intentional, Riddle thought. The man had difficulty with the finer points of etiquette. In fact, they all did. Jonathan had surrounded himself with similar types. They were machines, very good at a singular job, but one could deal with them as one would deal with machines: impersonal, without feeling.

Ganns proved to be of a different breed from Anderson. Waters and Wright escorted Riddle to the steel and glass complex where Ganns had his offices. Ganns met them in the foyer. He wore J. Press, a touch more flamboyant than Brooks. Jamie had to smile. He led them to a modern office that looked over the city on two sides through thermo-plate glass. A modern secretary with interesting legs looked dreamily at Mr. J. Riddle and his untold wealth as the party swept by. The humidity was controlled so that one was never shocked walking across the shag. Ganns made a joke about lost children back to the fold, and then smiled from his high-back leather chair. Jamie thought the joke had been in bad taste.

There were grey and buff folders on the desk. Riddle was to look through these, not study them, because Ganns continued talking, but there were photographs of mountain resorts and desert resorts and Riddle was expected to gaze at these while Ganns lectured.

They adjourned for lunch on a jolly note. Waters said something about a senator who was trying to push a Riddle contract with the government. Ganns likened the situation to the moment of birth. "We slap men like Fishbine on the back, and they start screaming for us."

At lunch Ganns' number one had also joined them, a lean gaunt man not much older than Riddle. His name was Jolson. He had eyes like a falcon, alert, hard.

They ate roast beef, began with sherry and moved to claret. Each seemed careful to drink well below his respective limit.

Again the talk was only business, but Riddle had absorbed enough to begin asking specifics. He said he wanted to know on what basis the foundation granted money.

"Your father had his pet projects." Ganns smiled.

"And I imagine I'll have mine," Riddle said, no smile, turning the stem of his glass between his thumb and forefinger.

Ganns moved to another subject, the operative efficiency of a new product. "It's a shame we hadn't more time to develop an effective testing period," he said. "It's a damn shame, that Nixon and his premature withdrawal."

Later Riddle understood that the product Ganns had been referring to was an infrared sensing device that had missed action in Vietnam by a few weeks. Riddle asked who made the device. Waters answered, "Westermark," and Riddle suddenly had an image of the African jailer lying on the brown brick floor. The man had died with his eyes open, blood coming from his nose.

In the end that was the memory which lent the irony to Riddle's goodbye to Ganns: "I'm sure I'll enjoy your service as much as my father did."

One might have said that to domestic help.

Waters, the executor of the Riddle estate, once attorney to Jonathan Riddle and now to Jonathan's son, loosened his tie for the return drive from Boston to Swan's Way. Jamie leaned on the armrest. He had removed his jacket and rolled up his sleeves. Wright, on the opposite corner of the seat, was an idling machine, listlessly watching the landscape stream by. The poor man was tired. Waters had had the driver fold down another seat so that he could face Jamie. They were to discuss the domestic management of Swan's Way. How was a gentleman of the country to manage his charge?

They passed a farmhouse, soon to be dismantled, Riddle was told, to make way for some government project, and a vision assailed him: he would be a solitary figure dressed in costly but unobtrusive habit, riding through the long shadows of a maple avenue. "Pleasant evening, Mr. Riddle?" the merry livery boy calls up, trotting beside the chestnut stallion. "Not too bad, Willy. Not too bad."

How was a gentleman to manage his affairs?

"Soames will regularly oversee all but the extraordinary functions," Waters was saying. "Under him each head of staff will see to their respective areas. Your father let him approve the budget, I merely passed it on to Poster."

"Poster?"

"The accountant. He's on holiday now, or I would have brought you round to see him. In the event of additional requests I was to consult your father. If you like, I'll do the same with you."

"With the nominal ones, you needn't bother," Riddle said, now getting into the swing of it.

"No, of course not," Waters mumbled, his eyes on some papers he had just retrieved from his briefcase. "However, there is one item here. Soames has asked for some additional funds to strengthen the security force. It seems there has been some poaching."

"Poaching?" Jamie Riddle as the irate squire would slap his riding crop against one shiny black boot.

"They've reported that some animals have been butchered. The gardeners, I mean. Jose, one of the gardeners, found the bodies of some rabbits and a deer. It just started a few days ago."

Riddle nodded. "Yes, well, give Soames whatever he needs. Can't have poaching. Won't do at all."

Chapter 17

IN the early evening after the meetings, the lunch, the signing of papers and the rest of it, Riddle met Carry under the loggia. He kissed her and they strolled under the portico where grape vines slithered up the trellis. They followed the red flagstone path clear around the east wing, through the camellia collection, past the pavilion with its canvas top shivering in the breeze like the skin of a giant blimp. They passed the white marble terrace where Neptune and Juno, Persephone and a dozen other glazed white busts sat between the sandstone urns on a long low balustrade. Behind them loomed the east wing. The detail of chiseled foliage, cut into the corbels and pilasters, hung in the twilight like icicles. Corinthian columns, fluted and fringed with acanthus sprays, were like petrified trees. Beyond that tiny world of stone and marble, beyond the tops of other roofs, beyond arches and bridges, gardens and patios, beyond all that wonderland that Joseph Riddle had his builders copy from a score of other classical copies, lay over a mile of perfect lawn rolling into the forest of Swan's Way. Which was a lot of land to patrol.

"I should turn it into a museum. That's what it should be," said Jamie. He and Carry sat on the railing, dangling their feet like children. Riddle wore a London Fog raincoat, the pockets weighted with oranges. Carry spat seeds into the grass. "I could bring in all the tourists from Queens or Great Neck, or wherever you bring in tourists from. Charge two bucks a head and then hit them for a donation on the way out. You know, put up one of those signs, 'Have you enjoyed your visit? If so, help us please others.' Shit! You'd make a ton."

Carry laughed and hung on his arm. "A Riddle through and through."

"Hey, I could have been worse. At least I'm willing to preserve some tradition. I could have come back and staged a rock concert here. But I'm not a hippy. I'm a businessman." He laughed at this. "I'm just saying this baby will pull . . . we've got a money-maker here. They did it with the Huntington place. They've got all those tourists marching through the library like it was the White House. If the Huntingtons can do it . . ."

"Actually, I suppose you can do whatever you like," Carry said seriously. "I mean it really is yours, isn't it?"

"Not entirely. The other houses are in the names of Sylvia and a few others. But this mother"—Riddle gestured with his free arm—"this mother is all mine. Can you imagine? Trucking in sightseers by the bus load? We'd arrange it so that they would plow right by Burt and Eleanor's place and Sylvia and whatever the fuck her husband's name is."

"Joel."

"Yeah. Well, you'd have this loudspeaker, get a big bull horn, right?" He made a horn with his hands and bellowed pontifically. "On your right is the house of . . . and at eight o'clock in the goddamn morning."

They had moved off the terrace and were ambling across the lawn. From a distance they might have been viewed as two drunken guests from a party that had broken up hours ago. It was as if they had crawled out of the bushes and were searching for their friends with uneven steps in the last violet light of dusk.

"But what are you going to do? I mean really?"

"With this house?"

"No, with your life?"

"What do you mean, what am I going to do with my life. Hell, Carry, I got it together. The world's my oyster, places to go, people to meet..."

"You don't know, do you?" she said with a wry smile.

"That's a kind of strong way of putting it."

"I'm not pushing you. I'm just interested. I wouldn't care if you wanted to work for the post office. But you've got to do something."

"Well, I'll get a hobby. Electric trains. Haven't had an electric train in years. Do the Lionel people still have the market on electric trains? We could buy the whole company. Build huge ones. We could run a track all over the place—"

"It's just that I would never want to live here," Carry cut in. "I hate this place."

Jamie's voice dropped to touch hers. "I know, it is a bit much."

"It's more than that. This house is a cliché. You know the story. Everyone does. A young couple moves into the family mansion. Strange things begin happening, bumps in the night, watery voices. Finally the toilets back up. The couple is driven by malevolent forces to madness or worse. But what's so damn irritating about it all is that the couple always just sits down and takes it. They never leave the house. Well, I'd leave. You know what I mean? You go to some horror film, and there's a crash downstairs. The man or woman gets out of bed. They start walking down the hall. The camera is zooming in close, right? It's focusing on the guy's hands or something. Then there's always that music." She did a poor imitation. "Then they do those weird shots of the hall. The thing is elongated and twisting like a condom. You know, to symbolize insanity or the supernatural. So, everything is building. Everything is about to happen. The guy is approaching the door, and you *know* that something just horrible is behind that door. The footsteps, the music, the camera zooming, it's all about to happen, and then you hear it. It's a little whisper from the row in back of you. In fact it's all over the audience. 'Shit! If I was that guy, I wouldn't go walking down that hall!' Well, Jamie, I wouldn't walk down that hall either." Riddle was laughing now, but Carry went on quite seriously. "I mean it. Not about this house being haunted. But, still, this place is fucked. All it's good for is melodrama. Why don't you sign it over to Aunt Stella and get out of here?"

"I will, but first I have to see something."

"What? The thing behind that door?"

Riddle shoved both hands in the pockets of his raincoat, and lumbered toward a small circular Roman temple. The temple was really nothing more than a ring of Doric columns supporting a marble cupola. It looked vaguely like an ornamentation on a wedding cake, except that inside was a statue of a naked athlete. "I want to understand what the power is. The money, the pull, you understand what I'm saying?" He faced her, a cigarette hanging from his mouth.

"Why?"

"Because, I have to know if something can be made out of it, something . . . helpful."

"What, like charity? Like the Jerry Lewis drive for muscular dystrophy? Oh, that would be wonderful, Jamie. Get your picture taken with Jerry Lewis. You and he, standing together, surrounded by—"

"That's not what I meant."

"Okay, so you'll give the money to the grape workers. Send them monogrammed towels to dry their backs after they swim across the Rio Grande. I tell you it's been done. It's all been done before, and it hasn't really helped anybody. Not in the long run. But then there's other ways to go. You can always climb into your father's cockpit, pop the clutch and drive right into the heart of that great money market of the world. You can even make more. I mean, maybe we don't really have enough after all. Notice how I say 'we'? Maybe fifty million, or whatever it is, doesn't make it. So, you can go to work. I'll handle the *good* works and you can . . . or is that wrong too? How about we just float through life, you in long white flannels and me in chiffon. You can wear those shoes from wherever they're from, two hundred dollars a pair. Leather jobs made from cows, that have been herded with feather dusters, so the hide shouldn't get mussed. We'll spend summers in Cannes, winters in Klosters. We shall entertain. We shall invite the Nugents. Oh, you remember the Nugents. They have two Ferraris, the interiors made from the same leather as your shoes. Feather-dusted cows."

"Come on, Carry, I'm just saying that there are things one can do with the kind of power that sits in this family—"

"You want to be a hero," she said kindly. "Well, you already are one." She laced her arms around his neck and stretched on tiptoes to kiss him. "You can do whatever you want, darling," she told him softly, pulling him down to his knees. "But take that out," and she tossed his cigarette over his shoulder. There was a tiny burst of sparks in the grass. "I told you, I don't care what you do." She undid the buttons of his shirt. "All I want is to . . ." She buried her lips into his neck. She was whispering unintelligible oaths between kisses. He pressed her into his body, and she responded, first melting, and then suddenly rigid as if cold. She said his name, but there was something wrong because it was a gasping little scream. "Jamie. Oh my God. Look!"

She fell back on the grass, pointing to something. Still on his knees, Riddle spun around but there was only the damp pale wash of moonlight on foliage and marble. Leaves shuddered with the wind, but not with the movement of anything living. "The face, look at the face." And now he was wondering how she knew about the face. Maybe she had seen the eyes, the glassy, vacant eyes. But they were gone. He'd blown it all away with Toby's remarkable automatic. So why was she talking about the face? There was no face. Except the face of the statue.

It had been a squirrel, or a rabbit. It was hard to tell. Its belly had been slit open and then the body had been squashed like ripe fruit into the marble face. Blood was smeared over the shoulders and chest, and Riddle's first thought was that it must have been a fresh kill because the blood still ran. The killer must be nearby.

Later he would think about what Radan had said about not going far enough down that road . . . he would wonder seriously if it was true, because now it was important to know just where he stood. That is, in case Toby had been wrong, and it wasn't over after all.

But his first thought was: the butcher is still near here. . . .

Chapter 18

YELLOW bees and bluebottle flies droned among the roses and azaleas. Sunshine streamed through the canopy of vines that followed the crosshatched trellis in a high arch above the red stone patio. Riddle and Max sat at a white iron table in the net of shade and warm light. The patio lay on the hip of a rise beneath the south wing of the main house, and Riddle had only to turn his head to see the whole expanse of meandering paths, sculptured hedges, the fountains and statues, and finally the entire plain of perfect grass, glistening like some magic kingdom in the morning light. But he did not turn his head. His world was reduced to cigarettes and coffee, and a half-eaten sweet roll and some of what Max was saying.

"I remember that your father had not been at all taken with Swan's Way, not in the beginning, at any rate." Max spoke with an archaic Southern drawl that made one think of white plantations, the droop of willows and mint juleps for the slow afternoons under the veranda. "It seems that your father thought this place overblown, somehow rather threatening, although I like to think that we had a very good time for a while in spite of what this house truly represents. Then, it seemed he became proud of Swan's Way. Excessively so. Do you know why he changed?"

"Africa? He had a breakdown in Africa . . ." Although at the time Jamie had not understood that men broke down and their minds went bad, so he'd told himself that his father was dead and a ghost had come to roost in Swan's Way, an angry ghost. It made sense. Jamie had never forgotten how his father's eyes had been sometimes. Of course what did he know . . . he was only a kid . . .

"Yes, it had been Africa, but of course they say your father recovered. And so I suppose we should believe that he simply found a . . . well, a role that made a place like this acceptable."

" 'Role,' " Riddle said silently. Normally one would have chosen another word.

Max rose and began to lead Riddle down the path to the gardens. They walked slowly, winding in and out between the hedges and flowers. "You know that Stella is upset that you and Carry have been sleeping together. What's the word for that? Fornication?"

Riddle smiled. He didn't give a shit what Stella thought.

"But you must understand that they're afraid of you, Jamie."

"Afraid?"

"Yes, well, they don't know what your plans are. They want you to take a firm hold on the reins, or not take hold. Uncertainty, it can be hard on these people."

They had stopped by a fountain. Jets of spray scattered by the wind broke the light to rainbows. So he was a one-legged sailor at the wheel of a storm-tossed ship?

"They're afraid of you, Jamie, because they don't know you. They don't know what you've done with yourself all those years."

Riddle, skimming a hand along the water, said, "I was a sort of soldier . . . in a way a mercenary."

"Oh? Well, that must have been exciting."

"Yeah, sometimes." They might have been talking football.

"Where did you do this?"

"Actually I was kind of attached to an organization." He should, he decided, have said team. Less pretentious.

"What were your . . . duties?"

"You know, they'd send you out on a job. They called them runs."

"If I recall, you used to be a bit of a cloak-and-dagger character at school. Always sneaking here and sneaking there. In and out of trouble. Weren't you even sent down once?"

"Sent down? You mean kicked out?"

"Yes."

"Yeah, well, I had a fight. I had a fight with a kid named Tony Archer." Riddle suddenly remembered that it was hardly a fight. Archer was head of a lot of clubs. He had a reputation for sucking up to the staff. He was also the Dorm Watch, the little creep. Once he found Carry in Jamie's room after hours. He called her a tramp and Riddle hit him in the face. Twice, once in the mouth and then on the jaw.

"That's rather odd," Max put in. "I know the Archers. Not the boy, particularly, but his parents. You've had trouble with that type before. Or should I say, afterward?"

"What type?"

"The Tony Archers."

"Yeah, well, sometimes it just happened," Jamie slurred, immediately realizing that he sounded like an earlier incarnation of himself . . . again the sullen punk kid, brought before a school dean who was out to help that problem child . . . only he'd never been a problem child. He was hard core, a real delinquent. It took a while for them to realize that.

"You know, I had my Tony Archers too," Max said, "but I went a different route than you. Did you know that as a young man I was a student of Gurdjieff? In fact, I stayed for a while at the master's home, the Château du Prieuré near Paris. How should I describe it? You have to imagine this Russian, Gurdjieff . . . well, among other things, he was a rug seller. He liked to have his coffee under the trees in the garden. He would often be seen in bowlers . . . that's not the point, except I'm trying to give you a feel for the period. The romantic aspect of it. There was a touch of European parlor seances, and a bit more from the mysterious East. Do you follow me here? I'm still trying to give you some notion of the ambience. It's important because it was during that period that I became swept up in certain . . . let's say certain unusual ideas about how and why people tend to live their lives . . . motivations, that kind of thing . . ."

Radan country, Riddle thought.

"What I'm trying to say," Max went on, "is that there are reasons for things that occur that perhaps aren't always what they seem. Remember when I said that your father had chosen a role? I think it would be even more accurate to say that the role chose him. Let's say that at some point your father was faced with two roads. I only know about the one he went down. Where the other might have taken him, no one knows. However, what he actually became is self-evident." Max paused. His steps became slower. "Let's say he was pulled into the tradition that had been laid before him. You know . . . finance, business, there are others . . ."

But he's afraid to say them, Jamie told himself. He's like a parent explaining death to a child. He's talking around the issue because he believes the truth is too upsetting. So why don't you just call him a greedy bastard and be done with it?

But Max was already plunging ahead. "You're aware that your father's involvement stopped here . . ." Max swept his hand and commanded the grounds. "He only cared about what he could call his . . . his house, his land, his son . . ." The words were rushing out now. "Your father did change, Jamie. Haven't you ever thought about it before? We have to face it, he wasn't the same man after Africa. Not the same at all . . ."

He knows, Jamie thought. He knows that something far worse than a "breakdown" had happened to Jonathan Riddle. Now, some twenty-four years after the beginning of an insanity . . . what other word to describe it? . . . the two men stood united in this recognition on the mossy flagstones of the garden path. No question about it . . . Max knows, Jamie thought. He knows, only he's like me. He doesn't have the words to describe it.

Max had taken a few steps further down the path, and now stood motionless, his attention fixed on the sound of shovels and flying earth that had just broken from the woods ahead. Riddle followed him off the path and through the trees until they came to a clearing. Jose stood beside a patch of freshly turned earth. There was a shovel in his hand and a pickaxe at his feet. He had already padded down the earth by the time Max and Riddle reached the clearing.

Max saluted him in Spanish, and there was a rapid exchange of words. "He says he's just buried a deer," Max told Riddle. "He says he found the animal in the woods an hour ago. He said it was killed like some of the others."

"Maybe it was killed by a dog or something," Jamie said. "Ask him."

Max did, and Jose started a long tirade, pantomiming the words by clutching his throat with his hands. "He says it would have been a remarkable dog, a dog that can tie knots. Apparently the animal was found hanging by the neck. It had also been cut up with knives. He says there's a maniac loose in the woods. He says that this is the third animal he's found in as many days."

Jose began to speak again. "He's saying that none of us are safe," Max translated. "He's saying that—" Max broke off to hear more of the gardener's speech. Jose's voice was subsiding to a near-unintelligible grumble. "He seems to be hinting that you have something to do with it." Max had broken out in a fine sweat. His voice, his movements, had slowed down. He seemed to be struggling to keep something down. Fear, maybe, Riddle thought. "He's very fond of the animals, you've got to understand that, Jamie—"

"No, tell me what he said."

"He asked me if it runs in the family."

"I don't understand."

Max grimaced. Twice he started to reply, stopped, then finally . . . "Father . . . he said your father had done the same thing."

Chapter 19

CARRY had a word for it: the Twilight Zone. She borrowed the name from Rod Serling's old television series in which every week some poor traveler would slip through the curtain of reality and plummet down into that murky world where the only law was irony, and the only crime disbelief. However, in Carry's lexicon the name meant a state of mind, or more exactly, the country of the supernatural. Not supernatural as in ghosts or monsters, but supernatural to create a vague disquietude beyond explanation. The Twilight Zone was not necessarily marked by extraordinary events but rather by the feeling that something hadn't happened that should have, or something was happening that shouldn't have.

Welcome to the Twilight Zone.

She conceived it in Mexico. She'd been traveling all night, driving through the desert with a friend. They were exhausted. They came on the hotel, a converted river boat. It looked ominous enough, marooned in the middle of the desert like some phantom ship on the waters of the fifth dimension, and when they checked in they found that there was not another guest in the house. The clerk sent them up to their rooms with few words. The dining room at the dinner hour had tables set with silver and linen for at least fifty people, but Carry and her companion were the only ones in sight. The staff floated about, inconspicuous as funeral attendents. The only information their waiter offered was a warning not to swim in the estuary. "The sharks come in at night," he said. But there wasn't any water around for hundreds of miles.

Hello, Twilight Zone.

The Twilight Zone was nothing new to Riddle. After all, what else was Radan's hour of the noonday devil but a commercial break from reality that tried to sell the Twilight Zone to all comers? But this time the uneasiness had settled in and wouldn't leave. It was like a lingering fever with no relief, and no change. It wasn't the epidemic of butchered animals in the forest. Nor was it the accompanying suspicions that filtered through the household of Swan's Way. It was more than all that . . . it was as if some kind of contest had begun. Riddle had no idea what the rules were, nor entirely the identity of the opponents, but it seemed clear they were playing to the death.

Riddle formally acknowledged the new dimension the morning after his talk with Max. He also realized "new" wasn't accurate, that he'd probably been there for some time before, and when he heard what Waters and Wright had to say, it became official. The passport was stamped: Twilight Zone. Stay: Indefinite.

At first it seemed to Riddle to be a repeat of his initial meeting with his financial advisors. He took the same high-back leather chair behind the desk. Waters and Wright again sat on the settee like stiff near-cartoon characters. The mood, however, was different. Waters was demonstratably perplexed and Wright noticeably subdued. Waters was terse. "Two years ago," he began, "your father entered into a merger with a construction company." He laid a buff folder with gold lettering on the desk. It read "Parnell Construction." "The title has been retained. The ensuing project involved a housing and recreational development center in northern Oregon. The project went public late last year, and your father instructed us to maintain the stability of the stock as needed. All in all, it was a firm situation. You'll notice I said *was* firm. I do that because something has changed. Something that . . . well, you should be well aware of what it is. In fact . . . what I would like to know, Mr. Riddle, what I believe I have every right to know, is why you called Mr. Anderson last Tuesday and ordered him to begin selling shares at a rate of twenty thousand per day. I believe that common courtesy entitles me to know why you have begun pulling the rug out from under Parnell."

As he heard himself answer, it occurred to Jamie that Waters was talking to him in a near-perfect imitation of a schoolteacher he'd once had. Also that he'd once gone to Oregon with his father, and maybe the idea had been hatched then. And how could Waters accuse him if Waters himself had admitted that he'd never heard of Parnell Construction . . . else why take the trouble to explain it to him? Jamie was also thinking that either there was some minor misunderstanding, or there was a real person out there who was trying to ruin him. Either way he knew at that point he'd entered Carry's Twilight Zone. His. And how would something like that even compute in Waters and Wright's collective digital computer mind?

In the end Jamie wasn't even aware he'd spoken back, although he must have said something, probably something dumb like, "I'm not sure what you're talking about." Something like that, because Waters had already begun speaking again and was saying, "I'm talking here about a very serious matter, Mr. Riddle. If you choose to muck around behind our backs, that's your business. But Parnell has fallen twenty points—"

"Twenty-two as of this morning," Wright corrected. Riddle saw nothing funny about the exchange this time.

"All right then, twenty-two. There are a good many people who are going to get hurt by this. Some of these people are going to get very hurt, and they're going to be very angry. If that's the way you want to play your cards, that's your business. But the order you gave to Boston is tantamount to stock manipulation, and in case you aren't aware of it, stock manipulation is a crime in this country. A very serious crime."

Jamie could have out and out denied it. He remembered that he had been with Carry last Tuesday. In fact they hadn't even gotten out of bed until late afternoon. That should have been common knowledge because a chambermaid had complained to Soames that there were champagne bottles all over the room, broken glass and the sheets were . . . it was like the last days of Pompeii. But suddenly Riddle no longer cared what Waters thought. He cared more about the reality of the unreal world that held its own explanations for what was going on.

"No one else could have made that telephone call to Anderson but you," Waters was saying. "Why do you think Mr. Wright and I brought you around to meet the man? It was so that he would become familiar with you, so that you could deal with him on a one-to-one basis. In short, that you could begin to handle your own affairs, call him and he would know you. Anderson is a responsible man. He would not make an order on a call from anyone."

"Well, maybe someone impersonated me."

Waters raised his eyebrows and shook his head.

"Well, somebody else did make that call," Riddle protested, and then, softly, "and whoever it is, is turning my life into a circus."

A circus? No, more a mad carousel.

Chapter 20

IT was late. Maybe two, maybe three in the morning. Riddle didn't care. His watch had stopped. It was a self-winding cheapo that he'd bought from a Turk on the streets. It was probably broken.

He sat in his father's study. Actually it was more of a den, a man's world of leather, tobacco and brandy. Not that he liked brandy. He had been drinking gin, a good amount since he'd gotten up an hour or so before. He should have left a note for Carry in case she woke up.

I'm in the study . . . trying to make some sense of it.
Love,
Jamie.
P.S. If you want to contact me, leave a note with the night porter of the Grand Hotel, c/o the Twilight Zone.

Opposite the desk he sat behind was a pine cabinet containing antique weapons. There were Daniel Boone's flintlock, Bowie's knives. There were also the stuffed heads of animals mounted on the walls: a moose, a leopard, wild cats and an elk. His father's kills. The eyes of these heads irritated him. Probably, he supposed, because they were glass and their stare was glazed, unreal but lifelike.

Like the eyes of the ... what? ... enemy? Well, that was going pretty far, because he and Toby had hunted down that particular enemy. He had jumped from a tree in the bright afternoon light. He had slid down a roof of hot tiles, hung from a balcony, climbed through a window, seen a man and fired in midair, tearing off the face. So how could it be that the eyes reminded him of that enemy whose eyes he'd never even seen? That enemy was supposed to be dead. Of course, the bullets had ripped apart the face, but who else could it have been? How could that enemy still be with him?

The dream had told him.

He and Carry had had a late supper of asparagus in mayonnaise dabs. They had drunk champagne. Carry mixed hers with water, but Riddle took a bit too much. They had fought briefly before going to bed. It was nothing serious. Carry had told him he was growing apart from her, that he had been distant and morose all week. She described him as being "intangible." Sort of fancy, he thought. Then they had fallen asleep in one another's arms. Shortly after that, he had the dream.

He remembered little of it. Mainly the landscape, flat cracked earth like the bed of an enormous dried sea. And there had been black fingers of dried rock. The sky had been purple or violet. He wasn't sure about that. He only remembered the landscape and the fact that he was not alone as he had stood on that plain.

There had been someone else. In the dream he knew that the someone else was his enemy, and the enemy had eyes like the eyes that stared down at him from the stuffed and mounted heads of trophies.

In itself the dream would have meant nothing. A nightmare; everyone had nightmares. Even the fact that the dream's awareness of an enemy's presence still lingered (that same presence he'd felt in Cairo and later in France) was nothing to get too upset about. These were just things of the mind, the mind only. The dream, the feeling that an enemy was out there waiting—that had no true link with reality. There had to be a bridge . . .

Well, there was a bridge. Tenuous to be sure, no thicker than the single strand of a spider's web, but it was there. Concrete, undeniable events.

The bridge had begun to emerge for him in France. There was the murder of Candy, then Eric, and then the hunt leading to a clap-trap room where pictures of him had been fastened all over the walls. But whatever had begun there was continuing. Less dramatic, but it was most certainly there.

The first event, according to his notes which lay scattered about the desk and on the floor, was the most obvious—Parnell had plunged thirty-five points before Waters and Wright had stabilized it. The confidence had gone out of the stock and there was even talk on Wall Street that the Securities & Exchange Commission would step in and declare a moratorium on trading.

Then there was the clothing. Two days ago a package had arrived from Boston. The address bore Riddle's name, apparently the merchandise had been paid for in cash, but alterations were needed and so the delay. The package contained a sort of jump suit of green velveteen with a long plunging V neck to the navel. Carry thought it was hysterically funny, Riddle too at first. He even tried it on, swishing about the room. Then he caught a glimpse of himself in the mirror. The damn thing fitted him perfectly. He might have stood for measurements.

He remembered the hit man's recruiter's—Blocker's—description of the "enemy," and his vision of him.

Finally there was the plantation in Nicaragua. Steven Ganns reported that he had received a midnight call from Jamie Riddle ordering a plantation to lie fallow two days before the critical seeding day. Financially it would mean nothing to Riddle holdings, but for more than six thousand native workers it was virtually a life and death situation. If the plantation overseer hadn't queried the order with Waters, and finally Waters with Riddle, it would have been a lean year for the natives. Nonetheless, Jamie had never made the call to Ganns in the first place.

One, two, three events . . . and three times, wrote Ian Fleming, was enemy action. Once is happenstance, twice is coincidence, and three times? That was enemy action.

So who was the enemy? Riddle asked himself, taking another swallow from the bottle of gin and then settling back with a creak of leather to return the stare of the heads that lined the study walls.

Chapter 21

RIDDLE in the morning: wiped out, hung over, trying to pull it together to meet the Nugents.

"I don't remember making the invitation," he muttered, looking up from the piles of papers that surrounded him on the study desk.

"No, sir. I believe Mrs. Riddle arranged for the visit. I should think your aunt thought it might raise your spirits to see an old friend."

Paul Nugent was hardly an old friend. Riddle vaguely remembered him from school as one of those amorphous types who define the average. His father had done well in hardware and Paul walked into the business as if he'd been destined for it. To complete the picture he married a college sweetheart, a woman as divinely plastic as a model on a Greyhound bus poster.

Soames arranged for lobster salads and lemonade on the north terrace. There was a setting for five, although the party consisted of only four: Nugent, his wife, Carry and Jamie Riddle. The first three were already seated when Riddle finally made his appearance. Nugent was working at humor in loud, clipped sentences, his head tilted back when he spoke so that his words sprayed up and out. Nugent's wife was laughing, while Carry shot nervous glances at the door. Eventually Riddle was standing there.

Nugent, perhaps realizing that Carry had lost interest, stopped talking. The next moment all three were staring at Jamie.

Standing in a puddle of morning light, dressed in white trousers and a white blazer, the cream silk of his shirt a subtle contrast, he looked like a J. Gatsby on a Saturday morning with the world in the palm of his hands. Carry was relieved, knowing as she did that Jamie had not slept more than a couple of hours while going through nearly a fifth of gin. But now, with his friends about, fresh lobster on the table, he had risen to the occasion. Nugent stood to shake his hand. Riddle bent and kissed Nugent's wife on the cheek, a sanitary peck. Now it was Carry's turn; his kiss for her was as warm as sunlight.

But Carry knew that something was wrong. Jamie's smile was a literal put-on. He was hanging on by his fingertips. He was going through the opening amenities like a hospital patient greeting friends from an anaesthetized daze. He could fool the Nugents, but he couldn't fool her. She had awakened last night and found him gone. Afraid that something had happened, she had tiptoed to the study and seen him sprawled on his desk. There had been bits of papers at his feet, and an empty bottle on the floor.

"But he was always the bad boy on campus," Nugent explained to his wife in an open aside. "In and out of trouble."

"Were you really so mischievous, Jamie?"

Riddle looked up from the mess he'd made with his lunch. He had been idly stabbing at the salad with his fork, eaten almost nothing. "Mischievous? Uh . . . I wasn't really . . . I think they called it malicious." It was difficult to tell if this had been meant as a joke, but there was laughter anyway.

" 'Malicious' is the word, darling. I remember the time he

called Mr. Fothering an ass. Mr. Fothering taught French, and if I recall correctly he never got on with Jamie. Now I don't remember what touched it off, but Jamie called him an ass. In the middle of class, right in front of everyone—"

"It was *asshole*. I called him an asshole," Jamie protested, for some reason intent on setting the record straight.

"Worse!" Nugent shouted with a finger raised. "Worse still!" Nugent began tossing out names that Jamie couldn't remember. "Ashbury, the archery nut. He's on Wall Street now. So is Clemmit. Remember Clemmit, the cowboy? Wore his boots to class the first two weeks. Headmaster says, 'No boots.' Clemmit says, 'Sir, that's all I have, sir.' Oh, I wish I could do the accent for you."

Through it all Riddle was able to nod and smile, but Carry knew that he was at least a thousand miles away. Carry said something about Nugent's wedding, and there was a bad joke about shotguns. "We didn't really want such an affair," Nugent said, "but we had to make concessions. We even invited Jamie." No one laughed, and Nugent forged ahead. "But you were nowhere to be found. Took off to Europe, or so I heard. What were you doing? Let's see, that was the fourth of July three years ago."

Three years ago, July, Jamie Riddle was a long way indeed from Paul Nugent's wedding. Radan had sent him to Lebanon to spike a general who was whispering anti-Semitic obscenities into the ear of a local sheik. There had been trouble. The Israeli resident panicked at the sight of first blood, and Jamie was left holding dirty laundry. The secret police chased him around the city for two days. He couldn't remember how he got out . . . probably the soft route through Tangier . . . but he did recall, now quite vividly, that he killed a man by breaking his neck.

"Off on the circuit in Europe, were you, Jamie?" But all Riddle could think about was how difficult it had been dragging the body through an alley and out of sight. He had never been all that physically strong. It was speed, that was his real edge. His hands were like hammers, but they had to be moving. The body had weighed a ton.

Nugent drained his glass of lemonade. Carry poured him

another from the pitcher. "Andy was the best man. You remember Andy. He married that Nancy Lock, daughter of the police commissioner. Pretty girl."

But the word, police, began to bridge another topic. For the first time Riddle fell in step with Nugent's words. He was describing the village of Swan's Way. Something had happened there. Nugent had had to stop for gas. There had been clusters of men in overalls talking by the side of the road. Some of them had rifles, shotguns mostly. A number of the stores, normally open for business on Saturdays, were closed. "The place was crawling with police. Seems to have been a murder. I picked up bits and pieces from the attendant at the station. Ghastly really, and in Swan's Way—"

"Darling, please," Nugent's wife tried to stay him with a hand.

"No, go on," Riddle said.

"Well, perhaps she's right. I mean it's a horrible . . ."

"No. Tell us." Riddle might have ended the command with "dammit." It was in his voice.

"Well, it seems a little girl was attacked. A little girl from the village. She was only about nine or ten. And she was . . . well, molested, then murdered." Nugent finished with pursed lips, drawing sad circles on his plate with a soft slab of butter.

And if three times is enemy action, then what was four? "First blood," Jamie said under his breath. The fourth attack was first blood.

Chapter 22

BECAUSE he could not describe what was happening to him in concrete terms, Riddle spoke to Carry in analogues. It was frustrating for both of them. He wasn't trying to keep anything from her. He would have much preferred to have said, "Look Carry, the problem I'm having is such and such." But that was too much to hope for. So all he could give her was the analogy, and the analogy frightened her.

He told her it was as if he were drifting in a tiny skiff on a midnight sea. He was drifting further and further from an acceptable reality of cause and effect. Out there, on the sea with nothing but the slap of chop against the hull, he was having a real problem distinguishing fantasy from actuality. Later, he would say that all he was doing was giving her a euphemism for madness. "That's really pinning the tail on the donkey, isn't it, darling?"

They sat in the conservatory that lay hidden among the tall sycamores at the end of the garden path. It was dusk, and soft shadows of the early evening brushed against the darkening glass of the window panes and skylight. Carry was half-reclining on a blue velvet settee. She was surrounded by ferns and succulents. Riddle lay in the sill on lace cushions.

Carry had found him wandering in the garden. She'd first seen him talking to two men. Grey suits, close-cropped hair, she had known they were officials of some sort. After the men had gone Jamie had drifted—drifted was the word—through rows of perennials. Carry had led him then to the conservatory. He told her that the two men had been police. "And I think they think it was me."

"Believe *what* was you?"

"That little girl from the village. They think I did it. They think *I* killed her."

Riddle went on to say that he met the police in the game room shortly after the Nugents had left. He remembered that one of them said his name was Fletcher. The cops accepted coffee from a maid with nervous nods and then apologized for their presence even before they began to ask questions. Naturally there was no accusation, not the slightest hint of it. Somehow, it was assumed that police jurisdiction did not extend to circles where the likes of Riddle moved. Instead, Fletcher asked about the recent animal killings. He gave no reason why they might be connected with the murder of the girl. He went on to ask about the security procedures of the estate, the extent of Riddle property and the size of the staff. Half of the questions Riddle didn't even know the answers to, but he realized it had been immaterial to Fletcher. The man had really come to see Riddle, not to question him. Fletcher only wanted to get a feel of him. If he wanted to find out about the estate he would have asked Soames. Riddle had been through enough interrogations from both sides of the chair to know what Fletcher wanted. "No cop, even an ex-preppie from Boston, is going to try and arrest me unless he's damn sure he's got something he can make stick."

"Jamie that's crazy. That—"

"You're right, it's crazy. But you know why I'm so sure he actually believed I did it? He said there was a witness to the killing. Somehow I *know* that the real murderer had taken the trouble to make it look like it was me. Don't ask how he did that, or even how I know it, because that's the whole point of what I'm trying to tell you. I'm beginning to get these damn feelings ... more and more ... this sense of ... a presence. I don't know any other way to describe it. Things are just happening and they're getting closer and closer to me. It's as if I'm really doing them. Who else could have made phone calls to my brokers? Who else could have done any of this shit? I mean that's a logical question, isn't it? You know I'm not asking for the impossible. I'm just looking at a series of incidents that point to a conclusion and I'm saying who else could be doing it? Uh? You know? Come on, Carry, why don't you give me an answer? What's wrong? You getting a little freaked, is that it? Right?"

"Jamie, stop it!"

Riddle's next words came rushing out. "Insanity, that's what it really comes down to, doesn't it? I'm talking about *real* craziness here. This is the American Psychiatric Association stamped and approved bottled essence. No pleasant neurotics here. We're talking about the stark raving variety. Because if you want answers to my questions then that may be the only place you're going to get them from. So we can either talk about what's been going on down here in my terms, or we can just forget it. I've already been through the other possibilities. What do you think I was doing up there in the study night after night? Uh? Do you know? Well, I've been trying to make some sense out of it. The manipulation of the stocks, the butchered animals, now this little girl, even that faggy jump suit . . . they're all connected." He could have also mentioned what had, astonishingly, been written on the mirrors, first with Candy d'Light, but Jamie did not want to drag that one up in front of Carry. "I've got to face it, because don't you see what all this is leading to?"

Carry gave a violent shake of blond hair. "Well . . . it would seem that somebody is out there . . . I mean, I've only seen glimpses of him, second-hand descriptions, my own imagination, but he's close, very damn close. Can you understand that? It's the boogy-man come back to get me. He knows me. Knows all my secrets, every last one of them. That boy has done his homework. This here is no amateur. This boy has really got my number. That's why we can't throw out the possibility that . . . I'm trying to say that . . . maybe the only answer is that it *is* me who's doing all of it. He couldn't have just read the shit he knows about me, he's got to have—"

Carry had to scream at him to make him stop, and then the room was ringing with silence, like a cathedral after a peal of bells. Now he was watching her, mouth slightly open, eyes ringed with red. His face looked bruised and puffy. Finally he said, "Do you remember, Carry, when you told me that if we were in love we would always hate the same enemies? Well, now I've got an enemy."

He added, only to himself, "and God help me."

Chapter 23

APPARENTLY it was the magazine that sent Riddle storming from Swan's Way. Soames attributed its delivery to a postal error, but the subscription slip bore James Riddle's name. It was nothing Soames couldn't have rectified with a phone call, and so Riddle's reaction to a mild piece of pornography left him nonplussed.

Riddle and Carry had returned slowly from the conservatory. She had run out of questions, he of answers. They had shuffled in silence along the darkening paths. Flaming cataracts of the sun's setting light were displayed through the tops of trees. Before they passed through the doors, Carry made one last attempt to reach him. "One's lover," she told him, "should also be one's best friend. So why won't you let me help, Jamie?" He side-stepped the question and predictably returned to the study.

In his absence the study had been cleaned. Soames had neatly stacked the mail on his desk. There was a request for donations to the March of Dimes. There were invitations to parties from people he didn't know. There were two or three business letters he would forward to Waters and Wright, and then there was the magazine.

He had seen a copy of the magazine before. It had been in the London apartment of a Swiss diamond merchant who had a penchant for young boys under the age of sixteen.

At first only faintly annoyed, Riddle began flipping through the pages. There was a photograph of a naked weightlifter, slick and greased. There were young boys, smooth as trout, with half-smiles or supercilious grins.

Riddle rang for Soames. First only once, and then as the image of a languorous pale hand with red nails gliding across a boy's bare skin materialized, more violently. When Soames entered there were a few pages from the magazine at Riddle's feet.

"I want to know who sent for this?" Riddle held out a handful of crumpled glossy sheets.

Soames, solicitous diplomat, said, "I wouldn't know, sir. However, the addressed stamp bears your name."

"Don't you think I can see that? I want to know who subscribed to this, because it wasn't me. And don't shake your head at me, Soames. Don't give me that look. I don't need that, man."

"I'll look into it, sir."

The door eased shut with a muffled brush against the rug, and a final double click. Riddle stood like a beaten runner, strangely breathless. His head was down. His arms hung apelike. The glossy pages lay around him. A minute passed. He didn't move, but he knew that he soon would. Move. Get out . . . get out of here. He had to get out of the house, because the study had suddenly become unbearable, and not just the study, but the hallway, the library, in fact all of it.

Moving through the house, Riddle was like a sounding whale running for wide open water at the bottom of the ocean. And if a whale, he thought, then a killer whale. Spent your life learning the role from Radan, studying every move. So who's the prey this time? Who's the enemy?

He swept past two maids at the stairwell. One of them said

good evening, and Riddle nodded out of habit. Five minutes later he took a Jaguar from the fleet of cars in the garage. It stalled once in the drive when he popped the clutch. Never did learn how to drive properly, too much time in the back seat of chauffeured limos, Toby used to say. But now he got it started again and was roaring flat out for the borders of Swan's Way. He only vaguely knew that he was headed for the village.

In town Riddle found a bar, a dark, sullen place that smelled of wet zinc and cigarette smoke. A husky truck driver punched out melancholy country ballads by Linda Ronstadt, then sashayed with a vision of her back to his table of friends. Riddle found a place in the corner where there was hardly any light. He called for a whiskey sour, then another and finally settled into sipping a third. Two men in Pendletons compared notes on the murder of the little girl. "It's the Zodiac Killer. Ever hear of the Zodiac Killer? He kills at certain times by the charts . . . you know, like astrology charts." The other was nodding slowly into his beer. When the whiskey began to work, Riddle left. He was too tired to drink, and he knew that drink would drag him to sleep, so he began to walk.

The streets were deserted. It was fear, he thought. Fear of a killer loose keeps people off the streets at night. He was prowling through an older section of the village now. In places where the pavement had worn away there were bricks that had been laid two hundred years before. The facings of the gray-stone buildings were chipped and smeared with soot. Someone had written four letter words in the dust of a storefront window. He passed a cannon that had been rusting since the Civil War on a grimy marble slab. The streets narrowed. The buildings closed in on him like the walls of a tunnel. Blackness consumed all but the pale showers of light from the intermittent street lamps.

He rounded a corner and plunged into the constricting gloom of a narrow alley. The whiskey had begun to work, and he moved unsteadily over the rough bricks. There was refuse scattered about. There was the smell of rotting garbage; rat's alley all over again.

The slashed gorge between two tall buildings, the darkness, the three drinks . . . at first he thought it was these that set his mind scrambling to desperate conclusions. Because like a rat that had slithered out and was rearing in his path, the presence seemed with him again. He felt it. There was another behind him. *You're going to meet him in this alley.*

He took eight more steps and still could not shake the feeling. Someone had followed him from the bar, and now that someone was very close, twenty, thirty yards behind him, no more.

He glanced back over his shoulder, saw nothing through the spikes of shadows but still he was sure someone was there. He imagined stopping where he was, whirling around in the center of the alley. He would stand half-crouched, arms in front, swaying a little as Radan had said he must always move before an attack. Then he would call out, "Who's there?" Which would push things to a climax.

He kept on walking. He did not turn around. He would not be swept away. Not by any vague premonitions, by voices in the night, by any of those blabbering freaks from the sideshow Twilight Zone revue.

But you've already been swept away, he told himself. You're plunging through the rapids and heading for the falls, because there really was someone behind him, and in the space of his own steps he heard the telltale clap of another leather sole on the brick.

Riddle stopped, spun around. Up the alley there were shadows moving, the scuffling of footsteps, and finally the figure of a man stepped out.

Riddle froze, half-crouched, arms slightly bent, wavering between feelings of certainty and hallucination. Yes, this could be the moment . . . what had begun in France was going to climax now . . . at last the damn boogy-man was going to show his face.

Riddle turned and prepared, while his nemesis . . . yes, it was the right word . . . hovered in the shadows. They were squared off, though their faces were obscured from one another.

And then, "Why not try to finish it, Riddlleerr?"

"Who the hell *are* you?"

To answer, the figure stepped forward closer to the light and Riddle glimpsed the face. It was as he had imagined it would be. The skin was death white, the lips moist red. The eyes were mascaraed . . . and wide and disembodied and staring, like the eyes of the trophies.

The vision held him for a full second. Then the lips of the figure began to round over words like a clown's. "Try and finish it, lover."

Riddle moved in cautiously, circling so his back brushed against the dirty facing of the alley wall. The figure turned from a pivot in the mesh of darkness. A foot slid on the bricks. One of them was breathing very loudly. Something glinted along the leg of the figure. Predictably, it was the sword now being brought into play.

Riddle slowly feinted first to the left, then back and to the right. One hand was raised parallel to his waist, palm down; the other, passing over the first, was the diverting screen, like the passing of a magician's hat. You never knew which hand would strike. He had practiced a thousand times, honed it down to the near-perfect dance. By now the moves were innate. Instinct would ride him into the kill.

But this enemy was good, very damn good. Riddle swung in low, kicking out for the figure's legs. What he met were the shadows. Then the sword swung down, and Riddle just managed to roll beneath the blade. He was off his feet, scampering across the bricks. He got one more glimpse of the face, its eyes wild. And then it broke and started running back down the alley.

Riddle was up now too, sprinting after him. But the figure was very fast. The hunt had broken down to a chase, and both were locked into it. There was the pounding of footsteps, the sharp gasp of breath. Riddle ducked his head and started pumping, but the distance would not decrease. Ahead, the figure slowed to spin around a brick wall. Riddle rushed after it, but it was gone and now he was only following the slap of steps down the narrow dark street. And in that sprint it was a quiet time out of time, as if there was no speed at all.

There was, though, something like a realization beginning, a slow leak in an undifferentiated bundle of memories. That face, Riddle thought . . . he'd seen it before. Around another corner the figure was now darting up a staircase that climbed the front of a windowless brown warehouse. At the top of the stairs a door opened and then shut. That face will be waiting behind the door at the stairs. Go up there and you'll see it again, and if you can hold it with your eyes for one more clear second, you'll know. But he was already beginning to know . . . "I wouldn't go down that hall," Carry had said. Go down that hall, or up those stairs, open that door and that's where a ghost waits.

Riddle began to move. He was at the first landing. Very slowly now, open the door. Everyone in the theater should be clutching their seats at this point. "Hey, I wouldn't go down there, would you go down there?" a little comical voice ran on. Very funny.

It was a large room, quite dark. Riddle could make out vague mountains of packing crates piled to the ceiling. "Hey, I can't watch this, tell me what's happening," the scared comic inside him continued. He moved forward. This is where the boxes come crashing down, he thought, but there was only silence.

At the rear of the warehouse was a row of small windows, and he told himself to stay out of the light . . . stay low, stay near the piles of crates, and then a thought hitched on . . . Wanna be reminded of death? Just keep coming, sucker . . .

Ten more feet into the valley of packing crates, and Riddle stopped cold. The figure, a foggy silhouette, was simply standing in the corner. He's going to step into the shaft of light from the window, and it's going to be just fucking scary, the inner voice narrated. But there was no movement at all. Riddle could have attacked, but the figure just stood there, a classic spider to the fly . . . Just try it, sucker, and then Riddle was talking to him . . . "Who are you?" No movement, no answer. He repeated it. "Who are you?"

It turned toward him, "Who do you think I am, lover?" And then what Riddle had begun to realize earlier was flooding over him, and simultaneously the figure was moving into the shaft of light. It was walking very slowly with a clap clap on the concrete. It was speaking to him. "Don't you *know*, lover? I'm Jamie Riddle." And then the face slid into the light, and Riddle was staring right into those eyes and now he did finally understand. It was his own mirror image. Radan had said it . . . evil wasn't the absence of good, it was the mirror image of it. It was himself. The features were twisted, the mouth red, the eyes black. But, no question, it was *his* face. And then again... "My name is Jamie Riddle, so who, lover, are you?"

It was closing in on him. The sword was swinging back and forth. Riddle could barely move. His face. He might have been looking at a mirror, but the image in the mirror would not obey. It was unto itself . . . literally baring its teeth, with a rasping breath, stepping right out of the glass at him.

Chapter 24

THE image of it remained. He was alone, but the image of that face remained. He lay on the floor of the warehouse. A tower of crates had collapsed around him. No, not collapsed, he'd pulled them down to save his life. At least he'd managed that much. The blade had been swinging in wide crescents. He'd backed up to the wall, which was a surprise. Since Radan's training he'd never been forced up against any wall, especially by knives, even long ones. But that face had done something to him. Just as now, the memory of it was doing something to him. He had been able to bring the wall of boxes down, and maybe that was what had saved his life. At any rate, he was alone. The boxes had come tumbling down between himself and that blade, and then he was alone.

Only it hadn't been just the boxes that had saved his life, it had been a kind of mercy. Mercy wasn't exactly the word . . . more a stay, a stay of execution. He was alive because "whatever that was still needs me," and then he swore and punched his fist through one of the crates.

But the image still remained. If he closed his eyes he could see it hovering like an after-image of a light bulb that had popped out into the blackness. Once he'd swallowed a bit of Nepalese hashish the size of his fingertip and when he climbed to the roof of his Paris flat the sky had been alive with angels and flying saucers, and they'd been every bit as real as the face he now saw in the space behind closed eyes. So real, or unreal? Memory of an actual face, or hallucination?

He had gone on like that for an hour. He had begun to think of silly things: fantastic demons from an opiate netherworld. He'd once eaten half an ounce with a camel driver from the Balkans who told him, "Everything you will see tonight is real," and, by God, sure enough, in the morning there were three-toed footprints all over the Moroccan courtyard. Finally he remembered that twice a year the coffins in an Oesel graveyard were supposed to leap out of the earth. He'd even seen a man dying of a curse in the Congo. . . .

He could go on, and he did. If there was proof in numbers, he had plenty more weird events . . . like the baffling brain that solved problems from a jar, like people who never had to sleep, like a human blowtorch in Modesto and the enigma of the Shanti Devi . . . So why not throw out logic, rationality, throw it right down the drain. Now there were vampires and werewolves. There were ghosts who walked the night, and headless dogs who still could bite.

And there was that awful face, just as he'd always imagined it would be, imagined without knowing or acknowledging its identity. When the face had only been an imaginative mock-up, complete with eyes of a child's doll and those trophy heads in the study, it was acceptable. It had been like those flying saucers and angels in the Paris sky or the footprints in the courtyard, nothing that he couldn't forget.

But now he had really seen it, and he would never forget. He could run from it for years, run ten thousand miles, live out of cold water flats from Berlin to Baghdad, and still he would remember. He could circle the globe again and again, staying nowhere for more than a day, never passing through the same town twice, but eventually he knew it would all come down to what he was still trying to grasp fully—there was another Jamie Riddle and it was going to take over his life.

So . . . he had been right. There was a plane of reality that was not madness, a place where such things could happen. It had not been the delusion of a four-year-old child. He had always in his fashion known the truth even if he hadn't accepted it. His real father had died in Africa, and that other man, the one who called himself his father and beat him and killed the animals, that man had been someone else. "And now it's happening to me."

Somehow Riddle made it back to Swan's Way. He locked himself in the study, determined to hold out until dawn. Gin helped some. Not much. Every rustle in the leaves, every creak from the bending oak beneath his window sent him rushing to look out. Glaring out past the black hedges that cut through the mile of lawn like fissures in the earth was the edge of the forest, where anything could hide. He wiped the sweat from his eyes. His breath fogged the glass. Later he fell asleep, but morning brought no relief. Except that it was in the morning that he decided to begin the hunt all over again.

Chapter 25

HE awoke in the wing chair. Dust spun in long shafts of morning light. He could only stare into them. There was a muddled pack of cigarettes in his jacket. He found an unbroken one, but when he tried to use the last match from a damp book the tip crumbled away. So he sat, the cigarette unlit between his lips, gazing at the whirling specks of dust until he finally remembered. The intuition of a four-year-old . . . a very fragile thing.

"Your father has been ill," Soames had told Jamie as he led him down the hall to Jonathan's room so many years before. Soames had bent down close to Jamie's ear. "You mustn't get him excited." A minute later, Jamie stood before the bed. His father's face was wrapped in gauze. The mouth was a black hole. He would never forget those eyes.

Who could forget? Who could forget any of it? Six weeks later Jonathan took an axe to the horses. Out of four only one survived. Then, Jamie remembered, came a slow period of apparent improvement. His father's fits of rage subsided. Life developed something of an orderly facade . . . "And finally they've forgotten," he now told himself. All of them? And the quick reply that came back was No, Max knows. "He wasn't the same after the accident," Max had said a few days ago. Not the same person, Max should have said. Literally not the same at all.

Where was Max? Soames had said he'd gone fishing. He said he wasn't sure where, and for Riddle the next few hours passed as time spent in a dream. You're out of synch, Carry would have said, which Riddle decided was an appropriate description. He felt as if the world was moving too fast, or he too slow. He vaguely remembered deciding to try and find Max. He drove into the high land where the lakes were stocked with fish three times a year. He left his car by the side of the road and waded through the grass. He saw blue waters and the white bark of birches. He started at every sound: a sudden blast of wind, a scampering in the undergrowth. He tramped on to a second lake. The landscape seemed a smear from the glare of a sun that was too hot and too bright. Sweat stung his eyes. Insects whined. His ears pounded. Three or four times he called out for Max, but then stopped because he couldn't stand the echo. Finally he tripped and fell to the moist earth and the cool grass and did not get up.

When he awoke it was late, four in the afternoon at least. He couldn't recall having really slept, but he must have because how else could so much time have passed? He thought of Candy and how the time had passed in the bath while she died, and the panic came over him like spasms. But when he made it back, Swan's Way was strangely at peace—servants laying out silver and crystal; meat roasting in the kitchen; Carry having tea in the garden with Stella and Stella's daughter, Sylvia.

And Max was waiting for Jamie in his room. They made small talk. Max said he had only caught a few little fish that he threw back. Jamie asked if he remembered a fishing trip they'd taken together years ago. "My father wasn't with us," he added. There was an awkward silence. Jamie started to speak three or four times, beginning a word and then not finishing it. His hands kept picking up small objects, a lighter, a pen, fumbling with them and then putting them down again.

He's sick, Max thought. Why doesn't he say it?

Finally Jamie did. "Something's happening, Max. Something happened last night."

And Max said, "I know."

They sat in the lounge that led to Max's bedroom. When Jamie finally began to open up Max held up his hand, got up from his chair and locked the door. He laid out a bottle of port and one glass in front of Jamie and told him to go on. As Jamie neared the end of his narrative and began to describe the appearance of . . . "I don't even know what the hell to call it . . ." he was drinking more and more.

Max asked questions. He leaned on what he called "foreknowledge." He explained it as "conclusions you arrive at without the evidence of experience." He said it was a sign.

"A sign of what? That I've gone round the bend, caught the cuckooland choochoo? That I'm throwing away my own money, that I killed the little girl, and all those animals in the forest? Because if that's what you're going to say, then forget it, Max. I've been through that scene before. What I saw in the warehouse last night was real. That was my face. I didn't imagine it. I don't know how, or why, but I saw it."

Max drew a lavender cigarette from a gold case. "The Germans," he said, stopping to light the cigarette, "have a word for it." He took another drag and then went on carefully. "They call it *doppelgänger.*" Jamie picked the word up and played with it silently until Max spoke again. "It means double-goer, or, as we say, a double. The Germans are an interesting people. I've never been particularly fond of them. A dry race, really. At any rate, the Germans are not a people to invent a word that has no place in the scheme of things. They're very concerned with maintaining a precise language. Do you know, for example, that it's very difficult to describe a concept like *déjà vu* in German? They have no use, generally, for the unspecific. That's why I find it so fascinating that they have a word like *doppelgänger.* It adds *substance* to the concept. But, Jamie, for you and me and finally for your father the *doppelgänger* needs no added substance, no heightened credibility. Because, you see, your father, Jonathan Riddle, didn't die in that plane crash last August. He died twenty-five years ago in Africa."

Chapter 26

"MIRRORS should reflect a little before throwing back images," wrote Jean Cocteau. Uncle Max took the injunction to heart. "Real society," he was saying to Jamie, "has always been obsessed with its own image. Look at Versailles and its hall of mirrors. A narcissistic fascination from the days when the king could be told apart from his minions merely because he was the only one not covered with shit. Appearance becomes *all* important."

"Still, with all those quiet minutes before the pier-glass mirrors—mirrors bordered with laburnum and olive wood, japanned marquetry, tortoise shell or ivory—they never glimpsed the truth. The emperor has no clothes.

"The real society I'm talking about," Max went on, "is like the Great Soybean Oil Scandal . . ." It seemed that a Wall Street underwriting firm staked itself on a number of enormous tanks allegedly filled with the precious oil. In the fervor of buying and selling no one bothered to make a simple test by banging the side of the tanks to determine that indeed the cup ran over. Had anyone had the wit to do so, they would have heard only a morbid hollow clang . . . "The tanks, you see, like the society you and I now share, Jamie, were empty."

Max had banged the side of the tanks and was jarred by the ring at a fairly young age. "Twenty, twenty-two. At any rate, I was so upset by that dissonant sound that I ran, and before I knew it, I was floating around the continent on the wrong end of the social register."

To Jamie it all sounded familiar. But whereas Jamie was looking for a strength that eventually became violence (thank you, Radan), Max was hunting for knowledge, and his hunt went roughly from west to east. He first fell in with a group of fanatical Christian mystics in North Africa, then someone handed him *The Wisdom of the Idiots* and it was Sufism for a year or two. He spun for a while with the Whirling Dervishes, got dizzy as an opium eater and landed in Tibet where he was told that "the path to God was through the horns of evil." Not fully aware of what *that* meant, Max decided he wasn't quite ready to lie down at the base of Everest and so ran back to London, where Aleister Crowley was making a name for himself as the Beast of Revelations. Crowley was an artful dodger if ever there was one, feet in hell, head in heaven, but the man turned so many somersaults it was difficult to tell which end to address. "Still, it was from Crowley that I first heard the concept of the *doppelgänger.*"

With that as an oblique juncture, Max began what he described as "chapter two for the essential brief."

Jonathan Riddle began to come apart at the stitching two months before Africa, he said. Until his breakdown, life was tolerable. He'd become lord and master of Swan's Way and the protector of old Andrew Riddle's interests. His wife then was a pretty girl with glowing blond hair and a hope chest full of beaten gold certificates from the Great Atlantic and Pacific Tea Company. She was a girl of breeding who served sherry with soup and didn't know the meaning of the word "cocktail." They lived in that never-never land of croquet garden parties with pink lemonade in palatial craters of blue-glazed crystal bowls.

When Jamie was born, the nursery was fitted with voile silk curtains as thin as the skin of a princess and the walls were illustrated with scenes from Grimm. On his birthday Jonathan greeted royalty from three nations on the great white river of marble steps while a nanny in starched lace wheeled young Jamie in the Barbingham pram from kiss to gracious kiss. For over three years it was lovely and affluent, and Jonathan was out to make the world a better place for everyone to live.

It was in the dog days of a dry hot summer that it began to happen. It started with little things. Jocko, a family terrier, died for no reason at all. Vandals, who were never caught, knocked the heads off the Roman gods that lined the grassy promenade leading to the chapel. A bunch of young fascists was arrested in New York with a cache of Riddle-made arms. At the trial their leader maintained that the arms were donated in a deal by Jonathan himself. Influence and money stopped the authorities at the gates of Swan's Way, but the scandal spread like the flu. Next, Jonathan was said to have pulled the rug out from under an old friend by reversing a merger at the last minute. He also began to complain of spells in which he did things, terrible things, that he did not remember. He said he believed people were trying to kill him, and he once told Max that a monster was living in the forest. Later he began to talk about a dream in which he saw his reflection in a mirror come alive, murder him and then finally take over his life. And finally he decided that he was going crazy.

At this point in the story Jamie said something, a muffled curse under his breath . . . "Jesus" . . . Max couldn't make out the rest. . . .

"It was Jonathan's psychiatrist who suggested the vacation," Max said. "Jonathan had always loved big game hunting, Africa seemed the ticket, so off we went. There was myself, Jonathan, and his two friends at the time, Carry's parents. Not Eleanor and Burt, of course, he couldn't tolerate them at all. No, it was the Weathertons, George and Karen. They were the only surviving remnants of *the* Weathertons. George received a bit from the trust. She borrowed from time to time with her charm. No doubt that's where Carry gets it. In those better days, I like to think that Jonathan loved them both above all others. He would have died rather than let Burt and Eleanor take Carry, but in the end I suppose that's just exactly what he did do." . . .

The party landed in what was then Mozambique. There was the typical flourish of popping corks from green champagne in the gentle light through mosquito netting . . . "We had two days of living it up. You know the sort of thing: white linen on rickety card tables set in the grass. When the ice ran out, we set off on the heels of our guide. He was a character, incidentally, a white South African who served as the model for half-a-dozen big game white-hunter heroes. With his string of natives he looked like something out of Jungle Jim. Oh, and he had this remarkable portable latrine with English country scenes enameled on the bowl. It took two men to carry it, and smelled like . . . you can imagine." . . .

Two days into the bush Max realized that Jonathan's illness was not something to be cured by a change of scene. The dream of the mirror and the reflection that murdered him returned. And something new had been added. Jonathan began to describe himself as trapped in another world. When Max asked him about this, he only said, "There's a desert . . . no water . . . that's where it thinks I robbed it." . . .

Max could not get any more out of him. On the third night Max and the others were awakened by a series of shots. Jonathan had emptied his revolver into the shadows. He wouldn't explain what he had been shooting at, but on the fourth day he began to talk about a tangible "enemy."

The enemy was only referred to with the pronouns "he" or "him," and then only as if in passing. Max especially remembered an occasion when Jonathan had spoken of "him." . . . Twilight of the fifth day, they had wandered out of camp together. Jonathan was drunk. Max made small talk. Jonathan kept taking more and more from a bottle of gin. Suddenly Jonathan froze. Max asked what was wrong. Jonathan told him to shut up. They waited, and when nothing happened Jonathan muttered, "He's out there, right now. Very close." Later Max tried to question him, but he sealed up again like a clam.

Four days later they moved into low country. The vegetation here grew like great waves above their heads. Vines strangled up trees, crisscrossing and then swinging down again. Leopards hid in trees whose moss-tangled branches offered them cover. They had been warned of snakes. It was like swimming through a forest of seaweed. The light streamed down through a canopy of leaves with an eerie green glow. The nights were pitch-black. More than any of them, Jonathan found the jungle terrifying. Their guide had told them that the best hunting was only a day beyond the forest, but Jonathan said, "I didn't think it would be so dark here."

Up to this point Max had spoken with remarkable self-possession. All the more so to Jamie because Max was no longer the Max he'd known as a child, the pied piper for him and Carry. Clearly the man had a wider repertoire, more dimensions than anyone had given him credit for. . . .

"Whatever it was that your father feared attacked on the third night we were in the jungle." Max took his first drink from the bottle. "Monkeys had run off with some of our equipment and so Jonathan shared a tent with the Weathertons. I recall thinking that it was for the best because the man hadn't been sleeping at all well. I thought the company would do him good. Since then I've gone over it in my mind again and again, I can't tell you how many times I've relived it, Jamie . . ."

Max had another cigarette going, and inhaled vigorously until the tip was an ashless red coal. He poured himself another drink and belted it down.

"There's a time in the jungle when everything becomes completely still," he said. "In colder climates, the steppes of Russia for example, they call it the hour of the wolf. I don't know the native word for it in Africa, but I'm sure there is one. It's a time when the insects are suddenly quiet, the screeching monkeys are silent. It happens just before dawn, and it's at this time that a man's nightmares seem most real."

Riddle nodded, because of course there was also Radan's noonday devil . . . His noonday devil.

"I'd never been awake at that hour before," Max went on. "What with the talking, it was all I could do to keep from sleeping all day. But that night I was very much awake."

There was no scream at first . . . Max described what he'd heard as heaving a sort of moaning breath, and soon that was broken by a rasping, grunting sound. Max said it first reminded him of an athlete's straining for breath. "This peculiar breathing, this silence, there was nothing else at first," he said. But then the volume of it began to grow. There was a harsh, breathless shout. No words, just a raw voice. By then Max was out of his bed and stumbling through the blackness to the tent where Jonathan and the Weathertons had camped. Choked grunts now began to sound like the onset of an epileptic's seizure, louder and still louder. A cry became a screech, then diminished to a kind of wailing, and Jonathan's voice finally was identifiable . . . "Oh God, *no* . . ."

There was a flurry of motion inside the tent. Max could see black shapes bouncing off the canvas panels. One end of the flap had been sheared open, eight feet from top to bottom, as if something had ripped its way through.

"I began calling for our guide but he was already up and running toward the tent with his revolver. I suppose it was fear . . . I've thought a lot about it since and I think it was fear that kept me from going into that tent. I'm not ashamed. That fear saved my life, because moments later the tent just burst into flames. First there was a flicker of light, larger than a match, smaller than a torch, and then the side of the tent disintegrated in flame. I was blown back by the heat. It seemed as if the tent had been drenched in gas. Remembering it now it comes through as a kind of montage, a jerky splash of impressions . . . There was fire, I was on the ground, the guide was reeling back slowly, he threw a shadow the length of the camp. And then there was another shadow, an instant blot of black on the red earth. It was Jonathan jumping out of that awful gusher of fire. His pajamas were burning. I remember tackling him to the ground and smothering him with earth. The Weathertons had no chance at all. I remember that I consciously tried to put them from my mind."

Max fumbled in his coat pocket for still another cigarette. His other hand lay before him on the table like a nervous white crab. Sweat had gathered in studs over his shabby grey eyebrows.

Remarkably, he said, Jonathan was not in any danger of dying. "Psychologically, though, he seemed broken, insisting again and again in a ranting monologue that he'd been attacked by an animal. He said he'd been reading by the light of a kerosene lantern, the animal had attacked and the lantern was overturned. He said the animal was a tiger.

"Which was not the truth. The truth was something wholly different from anything I could have foreseen . . . In the morning, the guide and I examined the charred remains of the tent. The Weathertons, of course, were dead. But not from fire— from wounds. They'd been badly torn up, a knife or a . . . we couldn't really tell.

"Then there was the matter of the third body. The guide didn't think it could have been so entirely burned unless it had been drenched in a flammable substance. He figured that Jonathan threw the lantern, saturating this third body that we discovered. I thought it a little unlikely but offered no other theory. I really had none, except maybe involving Jonathan's dream, which seemed too crazy. We decided that the tent had been attacked by a native . . . After all, some of them in that area can be quite fierce, or at least were at that time. At any rate, that was the best we could come up with. The body had been burned beyond recognition, there wasn't a patch of skin uncharred. Furthermore, the face was sliced up so no identification was possible there either—" Max broke off. He was rigid, now. He took a deep breath. "So we decided that the tent had been attacked by a warrior, I can't remember the name of the tribe. The guide had a name for them . . . Basso . . . Massoo . . . something like that, it doesn't matter. Because," he added quickly, "it wasn't a native warrior at all, that third body, I mean. Not a native, Jamie. It was Jonathan, your father. I think you already guessed I would say that, Jamie."

Max called the man that had come running out of the burning tent "the double," although of course he did not know it at the time. That came only years later when he had finally put all the pieces together. He used the term matter-of-factly, as if it were the man's profession. He said that it took weeks for the double to emerge from the trauma of his transition. "I believe that's unusual. Normally" . . . he didn't smile at the apparent incongruity . . . "the double has no problem assuming the identity of its counterpart, but Jonathan's double remained an undeveloped specimen for weeks." . . .

One of the first self-determined acts of the double had been to banish Max from Swan's Way. Then there was the incident of the horses, and the double took to beating his "son" Jamie, whose instinct told him more than he knew. . . .

Max then relaxed some and launched into his halcyon years following Africa. "I went back to Europe, took up painting in the south of France. I lived for a while with an Ethiopian, a wonderful girl who eventually left with my blessings, to marry an American oil executive in Kuwait. I had very little money but I lived well enough. Had a lovely house. How should I describe it? It was made of cloud-pink stone. There were large bay windows and blue shutters. On any day of the year one had a view of the sea, and I'd sit in the garden and sketch below a crumbling mosaic wall. From there I went to Paris, stayed for a year, then on to Berlin, Munich, London and finally back to Paris. In each city I tried to take care that my life would be ordered, placid. I never drank too much or attracted attention. I was disciplined, my nose to the straight and narrow, but not from art. It was fear. The fear that I'd had, and been running from, on the night of the attack in Africa had now returned. It had been buried deep in me, had driven me out of my wonderful little house in France, pushed me to those other places, London, Paris, Berlin. Do you know what those cities have in common? Well, that's a silly question. I'll tell you what it was for me. Libraries. You see, almost in spite of myself, I'd begun 'my study.' I just couldn't forget that third body. I could not forget the difference between the old Jonathan and the new. So I went back to the matter of the *doppelgänger*. It wasn't an obsession, not after the first year at any rate. I just needed to know. Now that I've lived with it so long I think that if it were all to happen again I'd be able to go into that tent, as it were. Now that I'm used to the knowledge that the third body was really the body of your father, that his double had tracked him through the jungle, killed him and drenched his body in kerosene to insure his identity would remain unknown. I understand they often work that way, doubles I mean."

What followed next was neither the stuff of nightmares nor of science. For the most part Max did his best to keep it academic—a pose that somehow had always suited him, Jamie thought, although it hardly mattered how he told his story . . . Jamie had already drifted beyond any realistic skepticism, out of the Twilight Zone now, out into a land of bleak cold plains where jagged fingers of rock were etched against a dark purple sky, and there was unmistakable movement in the shadow of the rock. . . . Whether the image was from some illustrated story on outer space, or a memory of the North African deserts coupled with the dream he'd had, he didn't know. Later he learned that Max had a name for that place too.

"Every man," said Max, "has a double, and the double lives" —he managed a smile at that—"to conspire to usurp his life." This was the prologue. It was German, eighteenth-century, although Max had read the same line in a three-thousand-year-old Zoroastrian treatise. He admitted that the Persian was suspect and his translation not the best, but the fact remained: "It's a concept that has been active for a long, long time." . . . Originally the double was conceived as merely an Ahrimanic shadow of the individual. Sir James Frazer noted that in some cultures it was believed that one could inflict harm on an enemy by striking at his shadow, the shadow of a man being his spiritual double. The notion became more concrete in the "Captain's Sixth Tale" of *The Thousand and One Nights* when the daughter of a king has to come to terms with a double to marry the prince.

The idea of a malevolent double appeared, Max said, in the Welsh *Mabinogian,* and later and pretty dramatically in some versions of the Grail story. Max said this latter reference was one of the first indications of the double's essential role . . . "The Holy Grail demanded purity, and whenever we see the distillation of good, the double has an entry into the physical world. Even Christ confronted His double. For every phase of the

Trinity there's an opposite—the anti-Christ, the false prophet and the Devil."

Max said he'd been at it two years, living at the edge of a park in a dismal one-room flat in Berlin. Everything was potato salad and sausage, little sausage men with sausage fingers and sausage brains, waddling to work, cramming into buses at six in the morning, faces fixed on the grey sidewalks. But it was in the Berlin library that he picked up his best threads . . . (There was an Alexandrian merchant in the ninth century who offered a reward amounting to a small fortune for the head of a man who could pass for his twin brother) . . . The other face of Berlin with its blaze of colored neon on rainy nights, cocaine and the shrill sybaritic laughter of cabarets was also an hospitable haunt for the myth of the *doppelgänger*, and he found others who were similarly caught up in it.

Max also admitted to some paranoia. "Three years on the trail did strange things to my outlook." He came to imagine a stalking presence, darting behind him as he came to and from libraries. Once he found a number of the books he was studying had been taken from the shelf in his absence. The clerk claimed he'd checked them out himself, although he swore to God that he hadn't.

But his fear had no climax, and with time it simply was subsumed in the research, which reached fruition late one night in his room in Berlin. He'd been working by the light of a naked bulb. His desk was buried under notes and texts. His eyes were blurry from fatigue. Small things had seemed significant for weeks on end. For example, a cockroach that he'd killed was still smeared on the wall, a symbol for something, he couldn't remember what. Then it dawned on him . . . it wasn't so much that he'd found some kind of key. It was that suddenly the *doppelgänger* had ceased to be a concept and become extraordinarily real.

"*Doppelgänger*," Max repeated it. "The idea of it comes best to us from Goethe . . . not that he coined the phrase but he gave us the first complete picture. He talked about the time when he entered his study in Weimar and saw looking brazenly back at him from the chair behind his desk what appeared to be an exact counterpart of himself. He called this leering image the *doppelgänger* ... It can be a wholly separate entity. Its function is to provide the human soul with a stumbling block—to dehumanize every human activity, to drag the human down into an inhuman sphere. Above all the double is anti-human and specifically anti-man.

"The double seems most likely to appear to challenge the possession of extraordinary lives. Men fated to make their mark on this earth also stand to meet their doubles. I've often wondered about the Hitlers, the Stalins ... that sort. Were they their own doubles ...? It would seem to be in the scheme of things. At any rate, the double is your opposite ... if you're good, then he is evil. He will think as you think, act as you act. If you can comprehend pure evil, you will be able to understand the double's thinking. And you must. Because he already understands yours. I've come to believe that in some dimension we all have doubles. I call it the 'psychic landscape' ... there's a place where the double walks and perhaps we've met him there ... But in the case of your father, and now you, Jamie, the double has come to occupy flesh and blood. For most of us it remains unrealized and intangible, but here, I'm afraid, we've got the real thing.

"No doubt about it, Jamie. He was born of human parents, natural birth. He was raised somewhere. He didn't look like his parents but this was overlooked ... after all, many children don't. He grew. And then there came the day when he knew ... It must have been instinctual, that knowledge, but he *knew*" ... as I did, Jamie thought ... "Yes, he was born for you, and you for him. But he has an edge because he came to the realization earlier ... he's lived with it for a long time, tracking you, learning you as he hunted you. But remember, he's human too. He has to eat and sleep. He has his weaknesses and strengths ... Which means he can be killed like any other man, even though he has no human soul ..."

Jamie felt suddenly enraged. He'd been living a life of tangible experience ... not exactly prosaic but, for God's sake, a life of this world ... he'd eaten creamed chicken, gone to the zoo; he'd stolen toys from stores, and taken tourists to the cleaners with the struggling-in-Paris scam; he'd seen a mystic walk on coals and scoffed at it . . . and killed men with his hands, and been frightened and satisfied by that. But now in the face of what he'd come to know, could no longer deny, all previous experience seemed to have been wiped out. *Tabula rasa,* clean slate. Jamie Riddle and the double . . . it was as if there was nothing else in the world. Nothing else of consequence had ever happened. They'd come into the world only for each other. Close as lovers, tight as thieves. Jamie was back on the flat plain now, the "psychic landscape," as Max would say. Call it what you like, it was another world . . . a place where Riddle and his double had fought once before. Jamie had won then. He had been the one born Jamie Riddle, the double was born Tommy Swen. Only now the double had come back for its second chance. It was going to try to recover what it believed was its birthright. Staring at the oval window, now black with night, he could see the landscape in his mind very clearly now, another dimension linking himself and the double. He was about to try to describe it to Max, but what could he say about it? He tried a few words, and all that came out was "lonely," which wasn't quite right either.

The phone rang, and Jamie had the abrupt, irresistible thought that Max would pick it up and say, "Oh, it's for you, it's your double. Want to take it?" He almost smiled at this, except that he noted the color had drained from Max's face.

"It's *him.*" Max whispered the words, one hand over the mouthpiece like a discreet secretary. Then to the phone, "All right, Jamie, if you want. The ashram. Twenty-five minutes, I don't move as fast as I used to. See you, 'bye." Then back to Jamie . . . "My hand is shaking. Will you look at that now, didn't think my hand would shake like this. Except it was so . . . I mean, he does sound so much like you . . ." No, he thought, exactly like you.

Chapter 27

POOR Max. It was one thing to conduct an esoteric study of the double, another to confront the reality of its voice over the phone . . . "He told me to meet him in the ashram, Jonathan's ashram, twenty-five minutes, what's the time?" . . . Max managed that much, but little else seemed to function. His hand was as though stuck to the telephone. He could neither move forward nor back. His face was red. A vein throbbed from his hairline to the corner of his eye. Later he would recall that Jamie had been remarkably calm, or so it had seemed. . . .

Jamie told him, "All right then, we'll go," then asked if they should notify the security guards.

"No! Can't do that! Don't you see, they won't be able to tell the difference. They wouldn't be able to help. They'll think he's you. No, mustn't do that . . ." And Max went on like that, backing stiffly through the door to his bedroom. He returned a moment later with a small revolver, a Colt .32. He held it in trembling disbelief.

Once Riddle had the gun in hand, Max began to calm down. He'd never seen this side of Jamie before, but it was plain that Jamie was at home with weapons. Max hadn't offered the gun. Riddle had simply taken it. He seemed to know exactly how it worked. His fingers moved fast. He had the chamber open and the bullets rolling out on the card table. "Do you have a screwdriver?" When Max took too long to answer, Jamie got up, rummaged around the room and returned with a thick-bladed Oriental dagger. He used a paperweight as a hammer and pounded a deep cross into the lead tips of each bullet. Max asked him what he was doing, and Jamie told him it would make the bullets expand on impact so that they didn't make just clean little holes but ragged, gaping ones.

Five minutes passed. Neither man spoke. When Jamie had replaced the cartridges in the chamber he handed the revolver back to Max, told him to wait and left the room. He came back with the most lethal-looking weapon Max had ever seen.

Jamie's words formed again in Max's mind . . . "ragged, gaping" holes. That was what it had all come down to for him. Years of disentangling a theory from myth, working below a naked bulb in a dirty Berlin room, and this is what it all came down to. Not a very fitting conclusion for a gentleman scholar.

Jonathan's ashram, as it was called, was built after a romp through Japan. It was a three-room copy of a Buddhist meditation center. White rice-paper and bamboo screens served for walls. The beams were shellacked red pine. There was a wide garden of white pebbles raked smooth three times a week. Beneath the grassy rise where the ashram stood was a creek with granite boulders arranged just so and a spray of fern, exactly as Jonathan had seen the Japanese monks do it. No one had ever used the ashram for meditation, although Jamie remembered that for a few months before he got tired of it his father would occasionally spend mornings there, brooding.

Max walked alone on the gravel path. His left hand skimmed along the bamboo railing, his right sweated around the butt of the revolver. He and Jamie had separated on the edge of the

Japanese garden. There was a spattering of dwarfed pines trailing down the steep slope of grass to the glen. "Take the steps slowly," Riddle had told him. "Never look back. It's got to look like you're alone," and then he had disappeared in the shadows of trees and vines.

The garden was cupped gracefully in the palm of a verdant dingle. Max on the split log steps descended into a flood of wisterias, camellias, azaleas and finally a swath of willow. It was dark and he had to feel his way down.

"Don't try to hide the fear, he'll see through it. Better to be nervous than try to hide," Jamie had warned. Of course it was probably the best advice, but still . . . how was he so sure? Apparently Jamie actually knew the way it would think. Then . . . "Whatever he asks, he'll begin by playing it small . . ." Now how the hell could Jamie know all that . . . ?

Max reached the bottom of the stairs. Ahead and up the path the vermilion moon bridge arched over the brook. Frogs croaked among the water lilies that lined the shore of an estuary. The surface of the pool was like black glass. "He'll be careful at first," Riddle's further insights echoed in his mind. "He won't leave himself open for an attack. Your gun is only for defense. I'll be the one that will take him." Instructions to the troops. Troop.

At the top of the bridge Max could see the ashram. The red-lacquered beams glowed in the moonlight. The rest was lost in the trees. "I'll be there from the start, Max," Riddle had told him. "I'll be there. You won't see me, but I'll be there."

Only thirty feet to the ashram now. Max was at the foot of the gravel path. Sweat ran down his ribs, like fleas. You're breathing like a steam engine, he told himself. Don't walk in there like this, it'll know. But Jamie had told him not to hesitate. Keep it slow, steady. Halfway up the path he lost his footing and the sliding grate on gravel seemed the loudest noise in the world. He moved from the sprinkle of moonlight into the smudge of shadows where the trees reached over the path. His fingers were slipping all over the pistol. It occurred to him that he'd forgotten which was safety-on and which was safety-off.

The path veered around a twisted pine, and he could see the

wooden steps and the bamboo facing of the ashram. The sliding door was open. Inside was blackness. "Jamie?" An awful thought began to grow in that silence. "Jamie?" *There would be no way to tell them apart.* "Jamie, are you here?" They would both answer to that name. That, of course, was how Jamie had known so much about the double's intent and future actions. Same mind, same voice, same face, same damn mind. And it was a cunning mind, always had been. Cunning and now dangerous. The young wolf had grown up with teeth. The wolf knew the difference between preparing a gun to hunt animals and one to hunt men. He knew how to slice the tips of bullets so they would fan out and rip through the flesh of a man. He knew . . .

"Jamie—"

Max called the name, cut himself off. Same mind, same face . . . same *everything* . . . a two-headed coin, and flipped end over end it could be impossible to tell them apart . . . *I could have been with the double all evening and not even known it.*

Now Max stood in the doorway. "Jamie, it's me." It came out a damn whine, and he wished he could have snatched the words back.

There was the trace of echo, and then from a black corner, "Yeah, Max. I'm here."

He tried to believe it was Jamie, the figure rising up from the corner. "There's no one here but us, Max. No one but us."

Yes, it must be Jamie, Max reasoned. Jamie said he would be waiting. He probably arrived first, and of course there was no one here and so he was waiting in the corner, in the dark.

Max still could not see the face, but now the figure was moving in closer. "So you saw no one at all?" It was the only thing he could think of saying.

"No. I see you, Max." A strange thing to say. Obviously a small joke. The figure was only a few feet away from him now. Max could actually make out the outline of features. "Yes, I see you, Max. You don't see me, but I see you."

Max wanted to say, I can see you fine. Of course his eyes weren't what they used to be, particularly in the dark, but still, he could make out the general appearance and it was Jamie all right. . . .

"But you don't really see me, do you, Max?"

Jamie was trying to tell him something. This was a little game. A little riddle. Some pun.

"You see Jamie, Max. You see your Jamie, but you don't see the real me. All you see is your little friend, but you don't see *me*, none of you do, but you will . . ." and then the double was moving in. Max stumbled against the rice-paper panel. One elbow tore through, and the ripping paper sounded like an explosion. But it was the wall across the room that had exploded. There the paper panels split like silk from top to bottom, and Max saw a second figure come through the gap. It was Jamie, yelling at Max to get out of the way.

Max couldn't move. The double held him by the neck, a knife up against his throat. "Try it, lover," it said to Jamie. "Please do come and try it."

Riddle had the automatic in his hand. He stood in the corner where the double had stood, shadows wrapped around him like wings of a bat.

"Throw it down, fucker," the double called out. "Throw down the gun or I'll cut fatso."

Riddle raised the automatic, and Max found himself looking down the barrel. "Pull the trigger, lover, pull it and I'll take fatso down with me." The double edged his way back to the door. Max shuffled his feet, trying to keep his balance. He heard the double's muffled grunts, and bits of ragged phrases between breaths. "The wolf won't get us, fatso. Don't you worry. Come on fatso. It's going to hurt. It's going to hurt beautifully. Then loudly over its shoulder, "Eddie, Eddie, come out . . ."

A man seemed to materialize in the doorway. Max caught a glimpse of him from the corner of his eye but didn't dare turn his head. The knife had not left his throat. "Eddie, take care of the one over there, the one with the gun."

The man took a step forward. He was black, tall with enormous arms and shoulders, but Riddle had now moved out of the corner and the man was able to see his face. His mouth dropped open. His eyes were wide. He's never been told, Max realized. The double has never told his own man, and now he's looking at the face and he's breaking. The man began to step back. "Get him!" the double ordered, and as he did Max felt the knife leave his throat. He jammed his elbow back, twisting free, and as he fell he saw Jamie, in blurred motion striking out at the black man like a snake. The man snapped back and went down flat on the straw matting. Riddle was instantly out the door after the double. While Max, down on his knees, watched the body of the black man thrash out its life on the straw matting.

Riddle found a clay oil lamp. He encouraged a sputtering flame. Shadows licked at the walls. Max still knelt over the body of the black man. Riddle sat on a low wooden stool. He had chased after his double through the gardens and down to the edge of the forest. He had told Max that he had been with the double for over two hundred yards, then had lost him. "He's very good in the night," Riddle said. "He's had a lot of time to learn how to run in the night."

Max didn't speak. Riddle said it was too bad the black man wouldn't be able to talk. Max seemed to think about this for a moment and must have misunderstood him because he said, "He's not going to speak, Jamie. You've killed him." The monotone in his voice actually was shock. "Did you see his face, Jamie? Did you see the way he looked at you before he died? He didn't know. The double never told him."

"So?"

Max twisted around. *"So?* You just killed a man, Jamie. You're ignoring him. That's important."

"He's dead, Max. I'm ignoring him because he's dead."

"That's not what I mean. The double never told this man because *he* doesn't consider himself the double. It's as if he believes he's the real Jamie Riddle . . . and you're the impostor. I don't know, but that seems so clear now."

"That's the only way he could see it. But that doesn't matter. What's important is that he makes mistakes. He ran just now. None of it was planned. In fact he doesn't seem to plan much at all. He acts. So far he's been lucky but tonight I almost had him. Next time I will . . . because he's playing with me, he's testing me, trying to calculate my strength. I'm beginning to see how he thinks, and much of it has no logic. He's trying to draw me out, the fucker. Trying to wear me down. But I see it, I see—"

"Jamie, for God*sakes* . . ." Max came very close to telling him just how much he sounded like the double. Mirror image.

Chapter 28

THE built-in familiarity with violence so much a part of Jamie Riddle was not revealed exclusively to Max. Carry too was beginning to see it.

First there was what she'd heard the detective say, the same one that had come asking questions a few days earlier. Fletcher was his name. She couldn't remember the names of the others. They'd come with a car of regular uniformed police. There was an ambulance to take the body away, a photographer to take pictures.

Jamie had said that he and Max had been attacked. He had struck the black man, the blow must have killed him. Jamie was told he would not have to make an appearance.

A crowd of reporters arrived. Max and Jamie answered one question in ten. It was almost painful to watch, Jamie sagging and stuttering from one phrase to another, with Max insisting there was nothing wrong as the police took the body down the path. Carry couldn't take it and retreated to the moon bridge.

There the coroner was describing the structure of a man's skull. Apparently this was in answer to a question that Fletcher had put. Carry could only make out bits of what was said. Then Fletcher was speaking. He bent forward at the waist. After every other word he bobbed his head. "I've seen plenty of cracked skulls. You're telling me no weapon, and I'm telling you there's got to be a weapon." The coroner tried to interrupt but Fletcher kept on speaking. "Smash a skull like that," Carry heard him say, "couldn't be that strong. If he didn't use a weapon then he knows a lot more about busting heads than anyone I've ever seen . . ."

Then there was the target practice. After the incident, as he called it, in the ashram Jamie grew painfully distant from her. He refused to discuss the attack at all, hardly spoke to Carry when they were alone and never in the presence of others (not that he saw much of anyone except Max). He had not made love with her in days, and then there was the target practice, less than a week after he had killed a man.

Carry had wandered out among the elms and copper beeches. There was a fresh carpet of red leaves, and the air was sweet. Black branches, wet and glistening after a midnight rain. She had gone about a mile into the woods when she heard the shots. First there were five rapid cracks, and then a burst of automatic fire. She watched from the edge of trees.

Jamie had drawn tiny circles with chalk on the trunk of a larger elm. He was shooting from the grassy banks of a pond across fifty yards of slick grey water. As best Carry could see, he hadn't missed once. When he fired on automatic, chips and splinters of wood flew off in clouds.

She had never seen a gun like that before. Sometimes it would shoot like any other pistol. Then he'd flick a lever with his thumb and it would fire like a machine gun.

Carry stepped back through the line of trees. With her hands crammed into the side pockets of baggy, faded denims, a green pullover sweater hiding all but a bit of red collar from a cotton shirt, she seemed vaguely pathetic, a friendless schoolboy prowling on a lonely holiday. She moved slowly over the leaves, head down in a loping walk.

Years ago she had told Jamie to "be strong, never let anyone walk on you again." She never imagined that he would take it so literally. If he had gone out and joined the weight-lifting program at the YMCA and come back as some kind of musclebound freak who bent nails with his teeth, it wouldn't have been any more astonishing. Carry had said, "Be strong, darling," and her lover had come back a killer. . . .

When the shooting stopped she stepped back into the clearing. Jamie was sitting on a log at the shore of the pond, smoking a cigarette and staring across the water. With elbows resting on both knees, in a long leather coat, he could have passed for a tired soldier, perhaps shellshocked.

For a moment Carry hesitated. She slid a hand along the bark of a tree. Then she called his name, not happily, but more like one might call a stranger, politely and with a hint of timidity.

"We've sat here like this before," she began. He seemed a little embarrassed. The pistol lay on the log by his side. Empty shells were scattered on the ground.

"I'm not proud of this," Riddle told her.

"I didn't think you were. I should hope you'd even be a little afraid . . ."

That last word stung him, and evoked a sudden vision of Erhart dying in the grass. Maybe that was just what he'd felt . . . Erhart died, and I was afraid, Riddle thought.

"So then why doesn't it stop, Jamie? The man's dead, but you can't stop fighting him even though he's dead."

He knew that she was probably referring to his father, and not the man he'd just killed, but for him the words summoned a very different picture, a vision of Radan. The old man sat very straight in a khaki jeep. Riddle could see the aquiline nose, the deep cracks in the leathery skin. He saw the sunken eyes, ringed with dark circles but bright like glossy turquoise. Radan's beard would be blowing behind him like the beard of a charging horseman.

"You've made your point," Carry was saying. Her voice was beginning to tinge with anger. "I don't know what you're trying to prove."

She went on to tell him that it was as though his life had

become a symbol, which seemed pretty well put to him. She said he'd stepped into a role a long time ago, likened his position to being in one corner, "your father and all that he stood for in another. You're fighting against the tension, the pull. Even though he's dead now, you still fight him. Don't you see what you're doing, Jamie? Where your father made money selling arms, you've made money using them. You've mimicked the crimes of Jonathan with your own." She told him she could understand part of it, but now he was no longer playing at the role of the rebelling son. She said, "You've gone right over the edge, haven't you? That role has sucked you up in it and now you apparently can't get out of it no matter how much you try . . ." She stopped for a moment, and then, very seriously, "It's destroying you, Jamie."

When Carry finished there was a curious lull. Like the echo of a single note, it seemed to suspend time. On the log, side by side, hunched over their knees, they might have been frozen images in a yellowed photograph. They were facing the silver pond. Carry's eyes were filling with tears. One rolled down her cheek. She did not wipe it away. Riddle assumed she was crying because she still cared.

The birds that had fled the crack of the automatic returned. One of them called from the branches above their heads. In a way she's right, Riddle thought. It's getting to me . . . hell, I haven't shot that poorly in years. Finally he said, "I'm sorry," although he wasn't sure that he really was. Maybe he should have said "lost," but it was more than that, and he realized, as she'd said, that he was still running away, and that the farther he tried to go the more he was pulled back. Carry said it was his father and all that he stood for. That may have been true once, partly still was, but now it was something else, and no way to tell her. Riddle kicked at an empty cartridge shell at his feet. No way to tell her about the double. . . .

Carry was on her feet, standing on the shore of the pond. The lapping water was soaking her shoes. Her reflection rippled across the surface, pale and incomplete. "Why don't you tell me?" she said quietly. "You know what's been happening here, don't you? You know who it was that's killed the animals, that girl from the village, too. Why don't you *say* anything?"

He, sitting on the log, she, standing at the edge of the pond, they might have been stationed like that forever. Carry's question would be going around and around like the snake that ate its tail. Why didn't he say anything? Because, Riddle thought, I'm stranded in a real no man's land, stranded between good and evil.

He couldn't possibly say *that* to her or anybody else . . . too damn pompous, for one thing . . . Besides, it wasn't his, it was something Radan had said. He'd come back from a run. He'd had to kill a banker who was channeling funds from sources untouchable to terrorists unknown. Radan had sent Riddle out to spike the man, and Riddle had ended up killing him. He'd thrown him out of the window of a London apartment building. "I can't see how we can ever justify that," Riddle had said. "Why am I any better than that banker? I killed him by reflex, for God's sake. Another man would light a cigarette with more thought than I gave to killing him."

Radan had taken a long time before answering. They had been looking out over the flat sands of the desert beyond Tel Aviv. The sky was dotted with stars. "Each pinpoint of light is an alchemist plying his trade in heaven. This was the only light from the dark ages," Radan had said seriously. Then the sacred doctrine began bouncing off the walls, Radan's similes playing tag with his metaphors. He conjured vivid pictures of thirteenth-century demonologists chalking pentagrams on the damp stone floors of Spanish jails. He stacked concept on theory until he had a wobbling tower with no top and no foundation. It was dedicated to some ancient Jewish nut like himself, and he called the tower "a governing law of good and evil." He spoke in loud, clipped sentences, as if he believed Riddle could only remember simple things. However, what Riddle remembered was that at one point he was ready to walk out the door. The old man was off and running through his cosmic rodeo, and as he went his English had begun to fall apart.

Then, Riddle recalled, Radan had become quiet. "It is easy to recognize good," he said. "It's evil, that's the bitch." He told Riddle that one only questioned the brutal act, the violent act, "the murder of an enemy, if you will," because one failed to understand the character of evil. "Dachau, Buchenwald, Auschwitz, what do you think I learned there, Mr. Riddle?" Evil, of course. "And to know evil one must be as God, one must have great beneficence. I have such beneficence. There are those who would disagree because they see that I train men like yourself to kill and wage war. They see that I train them better than anyone in the world. Look at your own hands and say I'm not the best. But if the truth be known, I have great beneficence. I'm a very good man. That's why I understand evil, because evil is merely the reflection of good. The left hand of God is the model for the devil. Now, you're stranded in middle ground, Mr. Riddle. You're stranded between good and the evil which apes that good, which imitates it. So don't come crying to me, Jamie. Don't come crying to me about what a rotten bastard bloody son-of-a-bitch it is that I've turned you into. You've left yourself wide open for all of it. If you're going to make it, then you're going to have to become a considerably meaner bastard than you are now. Evil doesn't have your foolish qualms. It is unqualified. Remember, Jamie, there is no middle ground if you want to survive." . . .

And now I'm in middle ground, Riddle thought. Radan was right. Fear has kept me from understanding evil. Afraid—he formed the word in his mind. Not afraid of what the enemy might do to him, he decided, but afraid of the day when he would no longer be able to tell the difference between himself and that enemy . . . the difference between Jamie Riddle and his double. . . .

Carry was standing now on the shore, digging into the sand with her heel. Riddle said her name but she didn't turn around to face him. "It can't go on like this, Jamie." She was still talking to the water. "Something is happening to us, something is happening all around us. I don't know who or what's doing it, but I do know we're losing each other. Things are getting out of control . . . Jamie, when you came here you seemed so strong to me, and now . . . well, I just don't see us making it, and it scares me."

Riddle hadn't moved. One hand lay in the palm of another.

He rubbed his thumb across the knuckles. He was thinking about his hands. Radan had begun by having him pound them in and out of dry sand. Gradually the sand was made more and more moist, until it was very hard. By then he could just about move his hands through walls. After a while they weren't much good for anything else. Once he'd been able to play the piano, but now his hands had difficulty stretching for the longer chords. He'd become afraid he might break delicate objects. He'd pick up a small object and wonder if he was going to break it. His fear of losing Carry was like that. Like her, he was scared . . . maybe he would somehow break her if his hands became too strong. Maybe Radan's concept of beneficent strength was just too goddamn divine for him.

Chapter 29

RIDDLE may no longer have been a hero to Carry, but he had not diminished in young Michael's eyes. In Michael's world, all that really marked Jamie as a man was the way he had pumped twelve BBs into the target. It was a standard of excellence to reach for. Michael wasn't sure he had the strength to cock his rifle as fast as Jamie, but with practice there was no reason he couldn't develop the aim. He practiced every day. His mother, Sylvia, had forbidden him to play in the forest. He told her he was playing in the garden, and then sneaked off. He had to sneak off. Commandos fight in woods, not gardens. Furthermore, he wasn't allowed to shoot in the garden.

Michael had secret spots. Places no one knew about, places where the trees were thick, and the leaves blotted out the sky. There was soft green moss on the forest floor, and the ferns grew waist high. It was commando country.

The morning had been hell. The enemy had attacked in full. Michael had lost three of his finest before beating them off.

Now, exhausted but triumphant, he reviewed the battle over a ration of graham crackers and a canteen of lemonade. He took one long pull from the canteen, throwing his head back to swallow, and caught a vision of the mottled sunlight in the net of leaves above. When he brought his head back down, Jamie was standing in front of him.

"How are you doing, soldier?"

Michael gave him a tough smile. "Fine," he said, and Jamie sat down in the grass next to him. In blue jeans and black sweater, Jamie looked less like a pirate today, but he was still not disappointing.

"I thought you weren't supposed to play in the woods anymore?" Jamie grinned when he said this. There was no accusation, just one rogue to another.

"Yeah, but I had to practice. Anyway, I can take care of myself."

"I'm sure you can. Let's see how good you're getting. Try and hit that tree over there." Jamie pointed to a thin beech thirty feet away. When Michael hit it squarely Riddle threw an arm around him and pressed the boy against his side. "Better, much better."

"Want to see another?"

"In a little while. Just rest here for a moment. You know, soldiers get pretty tired sometimes. Hot too. You're really sweating, aren't you? Did you have a rough battle?"

Michael was a little embarrassed by this. "Uh, yeah. Well, I've just been practicing."

"Well, you certainly got overheated. Here . . ." Jamie undid the first few buttons of Michael's shirt. "Better?" The boy nodded self-consciously, and Riddle pushed his head into the crook of his arm. Now his elbow bent around the boy's shoulder, and his fingers traced imaginary stripes on Michael's neck. "Did I ever tell you about survival training in the Spanish woods? They borrow the technique from certain African tribes. They can be quite tough, you know. That's because they purposely weed out the weak ones. They give you a knife and a little bit of water and then send you out and tell you to survive in the woods. Lots don't make it. You have to stay out there two weeks. And they strip you of every bit of clothing. Every single bit."

Michael tried to inch away, but Riddle didn't take the hint and held him fast.

"It's hard," Riddle continued. "But it's also exciting. There's something about being alone, completely alone with just your body and the simplest tools. It's difficult to describe, but it's really exhilarating. Like swimming naked late at night. There's a feeling of freedom. Understand?"

"Sort of."

"Here, I'll give you a taste of it. Take your shoes off." Michael kicked off his sneakers with the toes. Riddle pulled off the socks. "See how cool it feels. There's a little breeze. In the wilds your feet get to be hard and leathery. Do you know that the Zulu warriors run fifty miles and then fight a battle? And they do it barefoot. It's being in touch with nature. Most men are weak. They can't get to the resource of natural power. But for those few that do . . . why, they're our heroes, our pirates. Pirates . . ." He whispered it this time, and an image began to grow.

Riddle spoke of them steaming past tropical cliffs where the water was like topaz and the vegetation hot and green. The happy Jolly Roger was flapping in the trade winds of the southern latitudes. It seemed to Michael that Jamie was talking mostly to himself, and much of it he didn't understand. But still that idea of pirates held him and the lilting rhythm of the voice made him feel sleepy.

Michael let his head fall back onto Riddle's chest, and watched the sunlight burst like diamonds as the breeze gently rocked the tent of leaves above. Somehow all the buttons on his shirt had come undone, and that same breeze was like icy feathers on his skin.

Now Jamie's fingers were crawling along Michael's waist, fiddling with the snaps on his trousers, peeling them down. It was wrong. Michael knew it was wrong, but Jamie was telling him about the natives on the plains of Africa and how they would stalk lions naked and feel so free. Jamie had Michael's trousers off, and then the shirt, and he was saying, "Now you too are as free as the Zulu warrior . . . but even more beautiful, you are even more beautiful and more free . . ."

It was too much. The boy became a fish in a net, hauled out of water and kicking and twisting so that the man who said he was Jamie had to slap him and push his face into the ground, and now when he gasped for air his mouth filled with dirt and leaves. Michael, terrified, heard the breathing in his ear, and once when he managed to turn his head he saw eyes that were wide and dreamy, and fixed with hate.

Chapter 30

IT was Jose, the gardener, who found Michael. Found him more dead than alive, dazed and bleeding in the forest. He carried the boy to his parents' house, and then waited on the steps until someone told him to go away. Doctors arrived. They gave the child morphine among other things, applied bandages. There was talk that he should be hospitalized. Michael's father, Joel, was away on business. His mother, Sylvia, saw what had been done to her son and broke down completely, and so it was left to the child's grandmother, Stella, to take charge.

Stella came down from the main house in the back seat of a limousine. She told the doctors that the child would not be taken to a hospital, but if necessary she would hire all their services, installing whatever equipment they required.

She maintained order. The staff was doubled. Nurses were brought in. Soames sent two girls over from the village of Swan's Way and came himself to ensure domestic order.

But only a semblance of order that threatened to break down

momentarily. Even Stella, seasoned veteran of tragedy and illness, was not immune. When Michael's younger sister, who had apparently overhead something she shouldn't have, walked into the library and said, "Grandmother, is Michael going to be a girl now?" the old woman collapsed in a fit of weeping.

The police came back. This time only Fletcher and one uniformed patrolman. Over the doctor's protestations the boy was questioned. It was really only three words over and over. "Who hurt you." And over and over the boy screamed "Jamie!" But this was interpreted as meaning that Michael wanted to see his friend, because everyone knew that Riddle had not been out of the main house that day. So they sent for Jamie because he was Michael's hero who could shoot the Daisy air rifle faster than anyone, and knew all about pirates and how to survive in the woods with just a pocket knife.

He came alone, almost sure of what he would see. Stella met him in the library. He noticed that her hands were cold. She spoke in a low voice. She seemed to avoid his eyes. It was assumed that he'd been told what had happened, although the only words that anyone had used around him were "injury" and "attack." Even Max hadn't been able to bring himself to say it. But Riddle got the picture. Michael had been raped, beaten, and then just like that child in France, he had been castrated.

A nurse led Riddle to Michael's room. She walked ahead of him and spoke over her shoulder, giving the standard instructions. Before she let him actually enter the room she also said, "He hasn't been too coherent. You mustn't be disappointed if he doesn't recognize you."

The boy's face was grey and puffy. His eyes were bloodshot, and the lids swollen. Black stitches held his lower lip together. The shades were drawn. The room smelled of disinfectant and medication. Riddle walked to the side of the bed. He spoke Michael's name. The boy's head dropped to one side. Their eyes met. Michael's widened. The fingers of one hand began to open and close. The muscles in his neck bulged. His mouth gaped slowly open. Riddle saw the bloody fragments of several teeth, and then the boy began to scream. It was a high, searing shriek. It ripped out from deep inside his body. It went tearing through the walls and didn't stop until the nurse returned and led Riddle from the room.

Chapter 31

IF Carry thought Jamie in danger of becoming captive of a symbol, Max suggested that Jamie's double was also a symbol come to life. In a larger sense it was, he maintained, his academic pose to the fore, perhaps in hopes of diluting the awful reality of Michael's experience, the distilled essence of the bad blood in the veins of the body elite. By example: Joe Kennedy's last-minute dance with the Nazis on the eve of war, J.P. Morgan's feeding the farmers into the wringer for yet another dollar, John D. Rockefeller's even-handed screwing of everyone in sight . . . the double was a major character in such drama. It came leaping off the stage, swaggering through the aisles, thumbing its nose at the audience, a villain's villain.

Jamie was less interested in such cosmic interpretation than in the one-on-one as it affected him . . . "A symbol come to life" . . . well, Riddle decided, Max couldn't have put it better. The double was surely alive.

"And if it's alive," Max said, repeating himself and returning his attention to the immediate, "then it can be put to death." His words capped Riddle's thoughts. Max had found his nephew drinking in the study. Riddle had just returned from Michael's room and was going at it straight from the bottle. Max took one drink himself, and then got Riddle out of there. They took the Aston. Max drove. He followed the main road for a few miles and then turned off, winding up the hills to the high north pastures. They stopped by the side of a large pond on the edge of a marshy plateau. Riddle had camped out here once as a boy. He remembered a shivering night alone, smoking cigarettes he'd stolen, watching the lights of Swan's Way and the many lesser homes of the Riddles beyond blink out.

"I take it that you've killed people before," Max said after he cut the engine. "I mean beside the man in the ashram." Riddle didn't answer. "I only ask because it's important. The double has it built-in. They all do. When it gets down to brass tacks, that's how they must assume power. It can't run you out of your life. It must *take* it. See what I'm getting at?"

Riddle nodded.

"What did you call it when you . . . when you went after a man? What's your term for it?"

"We called it a 'hunt.'"

They got out of the car. Riddle sat on a fence post that had once been used to keep in sheep or cattle. Max sat on the hood of the Aston. He began to count the items off on his fingers. "He uses money like anyone else. That means there may be records. He might even have a bank account or perhaps he uses credit cards. I'm trying to tell you that these are ways that he may be found." The second finger stood for any clues that involved where he lived. "Somebody must have rented or sold something to him. Probably in the village." Max's third finger was for those who might be associated with him. "That man in the ashram, the ones you told me about in France, I should think they were hired. That means that he must meet with people. If we could find one of them . . . you see the point? Do you really see what I'm saying, Jamie? He is *not* a phantom. He can be marked."

Fine, Riddle thought. So his double had a checking account

and credit cards. He lived in a house, an apartment. Maybe so, but he was also a long-time resident of a foggy basement in the Twilight Zone, a place where basket cases like Radan had been hanging out for years. The double had squeezed through a crack in the scheme of nature, a crack that science ignored and Riddle didn't understand . . . "And now you're telling me to hunt it, Max? You're telling me to hunt the thing? Like a regular assignment? I don't think you understand. That was fine before I accepted what it was, acknowledged its special hold on me—"

"What do you mean?"

"I mean it's like a slow ulcer," Riddle said. He was picking at the fence with his thumb. "It's an ulcer, all right. It's tapping away my strength through some psychic pipe. You understand me? It's a symbol just like you said, but for me it's a symbol with real power. We're at opposite poles, my double and me, and no joke. Opposite poles of a kind of psychological circuit. And it's draining me. So if the double's evil, then what am I?"

"Jamie, it doesn't matter."

"If I'm supposed to be good, God help us."

Max ignored this and said quickly, "I told you, Jamie, we'll find it. We'll go on your hunt and we'll do it."

At which point Riddle almost said what he was thinking . . . It may be too late, Max.

Chapter 32

THE hunt began the following morning. Riddle and Max met in the garage at eight. Max brought a thermos of coffee and they shared sips from the plastic cup screwed on the top. They spoke very little. After they were waved through the main gates of the estate by a sleepy guard, Riddle mentioned that he'd had a fight with Carry. "She wants to know what's going on. All the coming and going. She knows there's trouble."

"Don't tell her anything," Max said stiffly.

"I'm just saying that Carry slept on the couch last night. It's a drag. That's all."

They were silent until they reached the village. Low storefronts; a hardware store, a dress shop, a cafe were opening for business. The summer was clearly over. It was threatening rain. The streets were quiet. Bits of white paper in the gutter, a yellowed sign announcing a bathing suit sale . . . the only remaining testaments to summer days and summer nights. Cold weather was coming and the tourists had departed. Riddle imagined that a lingering stranger would find the village of Swan's Way a difficult place to hide.

They began with realtors. Max saw three before noon. He invented a story that satisfied two, and when the third grew suspicious he fell back to the standby. "All right, if you must know the truth, I'm looking for my son. He's run off, you see. I believe he's somewhere in the area." The realtor confessed similar problems but still maintained that he hadn't rented to anyone named Tommy Swen or anyone matching the description Max gave.

From realtors they moved to boarding houses. For the most part these were once larger homes, now subdivided and rented out to men who worked in the mills outside of town. They got nowhere. Riddle became difficult. Small things began to irritate him. He complained of a headache. Once when a landlady, an old ugly woman in a print dress, told Max to mind his own business, Riddle called her a dog. After that, Max left Riddle to wait in the car.

By late afternoon they were prowling aimlessly. Max made a stab at restaurants and bars. No one seemed to want to help. A couple of men jeered at him. They gave up shortly before midnight. "He knew we would make a search," Riddle said. "He's been thinking ahead of us from the start." Max didn't answer. On the way back Riddle drove and Max dozed. The garage was locked for the night so Riddle left the car in the court. At the top of the stairs Max gave a half-hearted smile, told Riddle he would be ready in the morning to start again, and then walked down the hall to his bedroom.

Riddle paused. Behind him the red plush spilled down the waterfall of marble steps. To his right Max's soft tread was fading down the corridor. To his left was the long hall leading to his own bedroom. Overhead, the chandeliers had been extinguished. Teardrops of crystal caught what little light rose from below and threw a tableau of tiny shadows on the plaster mouldings of the vaulted ceiling. Further down the corridor it was dark, and rows of eagle claw doorknobs melted into the blackness so it seemed that the corridor ran on forever. It was still. There were only small sounds, sounds taken for granted, the ticking of a clock, the settling of the house.

Riddle took ten paces down the hall. Then he saw the light, a yellow seepage from beneath the door to his study, and he froze. There should be no light. He moved back and hovered at the door. Then he heard a sound, a shuffling of papers, his papers that no one had the right to see. He had a hand on the knob, now certain that someone was in the study. That was his only thought. Someone was in there. He turned the handle and the lock gave. The door opened, the hunt was over.

"Hello, lover, been looking for me?" It was sprawled in his chair, behind his desk. Its red lips formed an easy moist smile. It had a small silver revolver in its hand.

"Oh God," Riddle said, and turned his head away.

" 'Oh God'? Well, thank you, lover . . . I thought it was time we had a little talk. After all, what two people could have more in common?"

Riddle winced and his fingers knotted.

"Why don't you speak to your brother? Or perhaps you don't see it that way? You think I'm some kind of monster, is that it?"

Riddle was frozen. Fear took care of that. It was nothing that Radan had taught him to cope with. It had come in low, locking the joints, draining the blood from his stomach.

"Well, do I look like a monster, lover? Do I?"

"You look like me." It came out flat, passive.

"Of course I look like you, lover. You're my other half." Its smile vanished, eyes narrowed. "*Other* half, not better half . . . oh no, get it straight, lover . . . I'm not what you're thinking . . . not your inhuman counterpart. Not at all. *You're mine.*"

Riddle felt bent by the voice, forced himself to answer, "You don't *really* believe that, do you?"

"It's the truth, lover . . . the only truth for both of us. You have my life, you stole it, I want it back."

"But you can't ever be me—"

"Of course not. I'll be *me. Jamie Riddle.* I'm taking my life back. Can't you feel it draining right out of you, like blood?"

Riddle could.

"You stole it all, lover. I was born where you should have been born. My parents were ignorant, animals. They fed me hot dogs and meat loaf and boiled cabbage. Don't you think I knew what you were eating? Going to bed each night, probing your teeth with that little pink tongue of yours, trying to get that last morsel of chocolate. I know all about you, lover. I've known all about you from the start."

Riddle was trying to fight back, telling himself to be cool . . . find a foothold, but it was still bad, very bad, the fear was pouring through him and he wasn't accustomed to it. Once there'd been the fear of death, but he'd learned to handle that years ago. This fear was something else, clamping around his body like the suckers of a giant squid, pulling him down. . . .

"One night I woke up," it was saying now, "woke up in my dirty little bedroom between my dirty little sheets. That man and woman who ordered me to call them mommy and daddy were banging away like mules in the next room. The whole house was shaking, and I was lying there, and then it was as plain as the face in my mirror"—he had to laugh at this—"four years old, and I already knew that you'd stolen my life." The double was leaning over the desk, gripping the revolver with both hands. "I've bided my time . . . I had to . . . but now . . ."

Riddle had sunk to the floor. Like a ridiculous deflating doll, he thought. Soon I'll be no better than one, and he knows it. He knows what his power can do . . .

The double was talking faster now . . . "We are one person, lover. You and I, one person. We've been ripped apart, but we're still one man. We're a freak of nature, lover. Nature must have had a bad day, and we got torn apart. You know it's true, and you know what I have to do about it . . ."

But the only thing that Riddle knew was that his strength was pouring out of him, pouring into the double, for all he knew.

"What do you think I am, lover? A messenger boy from hell? Bullshit! I'm *me*. Fucking up my life, that's what you're doing. Mr. Galahad, Mr. Smooth, Mr. Spy for the goddamn chosen race. You gave seven years of *my* life away to the kikes. And now you're sleeping with that slut . . . You're totally fucking up my life, lover. What should I do about that—?"

"You should go fuck yourself." Riddle intoned the words. There was no anger in them, no energy seemed left for anger.

He was still down on the floor, sitting on his legs.

The double smiled. Nothing to fear from this legless cripple. "You're only going to make it worse on yourself. You see, lover, I can be a very hard person. I've learned a few things from you. I've seen you work. I saw how you worked against Erhart—"

"Erhart?"

"Yes, lover, I was there."

"Where?"

"With you. I'm an expert on you."

"It's been you all along—"

"Oh yes, lover, I've been with you for some time now. I tracked you in Cairo. I was with you in London. I was the one who came for that girl. And your friend Eric . . . I've known you for some time . . . sometimes in the flesh, sometimes not . . . you can believe in that."

"Yes, I guess I can."

"Good . . . and you can also believe that I'm going to kill you—"

Yes, he could believe in that too, only now his hand had slid along the rug, groped behind him and touched the plug that ran from the cord beneath the carpet to the only light in the room. Pull the plug, he told himself, and there would be no lights, and you've always been good in the dark . . .

"Well, lover, do you know I'm going to put your face in pieces, blow you apart all over these walls . . . ?"

And Riddle yanking out the plug said, "Not, *lover,* if you can't see me."

The revolver cracked twice, and Riddle dove to the side. He was up again, lunging at the fuzzy image by the window. He missed. His hand smashed into the skirting board and the panels of wood split apart. And then he quickly dove again, because another shot was sure to follow, and when none did he realized his mistake.

The double hadn't been trying to kill him. Not yet. Someone screamed, "Jamie," it was Carry in the next room. In a minute she'd be out of bed, running down the hall. The others would follow, and the double knew there was no more time left. He wasn't trying to kill, he was trying to get out of there, which wasn't very hard because Riddle was moving like an old man. No, it had never intended to kill him. It couldn't, not there. It knew they would all rush in and see his body. Not just the body, but the face. Carry, Stella, Soames, Max, maybe more, roused from their sleep by shots. They would open the door, turn on the lights and there he'd be, lying there, and the double would be standing over him. Their eyes would be going back and forth from one face to the other—and no matter how well the double carried it off, he could never really take over his life as he wanted. Because they would know, just as Jamie now knew. And Max. It was the same reason that Jonathan had been burned beyond recognition. Like his father's, Jamie's double couldn't enter his life on a threshold of madness. That would be a defeat. People would have to accept him from the start. He was going to have to destroy Jamie's face, his body, and he couldn't manage that with a small revolver in Jamie's own house.

So, he's been playing with me, Jamie thought. For now, at least. All this time playing, draining the strength from my body into his. And he would go on with it until there was nothing left.

Outside, the double had escaped into the night. Jamie stood on the porch. He had seen it round the staircase, head toward the door, but now scanning the lawn he knew it was useless even to try to follow. He was very good in the night. In fact, Riddle decided, even better than I am. Maybe he hadn't always been, but now he was beginning to hold the upper hand all around.

Chapter 33

HE *was at home in the night. They could send out guards with dogs and they wouldn't find him. They could scamper all night over the hills, plow through the brush, the dogs yelping, the flashlights sweeping the forest, and still they would not find him.*

He was too good in the night.

He was safe now. Yes, safe. Safe like the wolves in their den. Except he was not the wolf. He was Jamie Riddle. That other one, that impostor, was the wolf. Stole my life. Killed my boys in France. Killed my Eddie, my beautiful Eddie, killed him like a wolf would kill. So be it. Nobody left now but the wolf and me. The two of us.

He crouched beneath the ferns. The soil was moist and seeping through the knees of his trousers, which angered him. Now he would have to walk back with damp knees. Should have killed the wolf when I had a chance. No. Too soon. And after all these years he could wait a little longer. The takeover ... take back . . . *had to be smooth, smooth as when he took over* my *life. Tricked me before I was born.*

That was something he never fully understood. It was part of the dream, which was how the idea started in the first place. It was the same dream, night after night, year after year. There was the wolf and there was himself. They were in a place where there was only desert and black rock like petrified fingers of a giant against a purple sky. It was cold in the night and hot, hot as hell, in the day. They met out there. He could never quite remember the details, but he knew what had happened. The wolf had gotten his life. He couldn't describe it. It was something that he knew. The wolf had tricked him. The wolf was born Jamie Riddle and he was born Tommy Swen. *But I'm Jamie Riddle . . .* He'd been born in a place where it was hot and the people were animals, and he hated them. "Hate them so much," he said aloud. No, be still. Be calm. Everything is going to be all right. Be still. And he was, because there was a rustle in the bush. An animal? Yes, another deer. He hated the deer too. Just like he hated all the people that had ever helped the wolf trick him.

It had almost worked. He was born Tommy Swen, and he almost believed them even though he didn't look a bit like his parents. They were dark, ugly, brutish. They were like the cows they raised, humping each other, humping and mooing. Then one day so long ago that he could not really remember, the dreams started. He told the wolf that he was four years old when the dream began but he really wasn't certain. Who could remember when they first realized they were alive?

"Well, I can be easy now," he told himself. "I'm almost there." And so he was. Soon he would start the final phase, would begin to move further in on the wolf. He'd already begun slowly to destroy his power, and when he was finally groveling face down in the dirt, then he would kill him, and then he would pulverize that face beyond recognition. And then he would be the only one. He would be who he was.

He began now to make his way through the forest, wading through ferns and grass, cutting a path with his hands like a swimmer. There was the sloshing of his feet in the wet ground, *and the regular throb of insects. Crickets, mostly. Crickets were something he liked. "They're forced out in the night like me."*

He had once heard that their throbbing sound was a code. For those who had the ear, they sang the names of those who would soon die. It was an appealing story, because they always sang the same song: Riddle . . . Riddle . . . Riddlleerr.

Chapter 34

THE deterioration of Jamie provided its own chain-reaction. Riddle holdings began plunging rapidly across a broad front. Shares of Westermark, Horizon, and BBD&O, dumped on the open market, tailspinned in most instances to frightening depths. The avalanche began with the second alleged phone call from Riddle to his broker.

Riddle stood in his father's study. His shirttails were out. The palm of his hand was clamped over the mouthpiece. "I tell you I didn't place that order. I never told anyone to sell a thing."

Waters pursed his lips. The red around his eyes was from strain. "They've run a decent house for twenty years."

"Yeah? Well, what's that supposed to mean? That I'm lying? If you think I'm lying then why don't you just say it now?"

The following day Steven Ganns resigned. The Wall Street Journal carried the longest story of his walkout, quoting Ganns as saying, "I spoke with Mr. Riddle, and it became clear that we no longer were compatible."

Rumors in high circles held that Ganns did not resign but was fired.

There were other rumors. At the Stock Exchange luncheon club the story circulated that the SEC planned to investigate an incident involving a case of fraud. It was said that Riddle drafted a memorandum distributed to the employees of Westermark suggesting that they purchase stock in the company, and do so promptly. The memorandum indicated that the value of the stock was going to rise. According to SEC regulations, if a stock is offered to more than twenty-five people, it becomes an offering, and if the information presented to prospective buyers is untrue, the buyers may sue.

As the bottom fell out of Westermark, there was indeed talk of litigation. Riddle, of course, also denied ever drafting the memorandum, but at that point denials made little difference. "Rattling bones," Waters called them.

On the third day of attacks, Waters resigned. An hour later Wright followed suit.

There was more. Some of it was so preposterous as to be ineffective. Certain telephone calls, for example, to family, friends and advisors by a man claiming to be Jamie Riddle were dismissed as obscene jokes, probably from an unhappy Riddle employee. Others, however, calls to various financial heads of Riddle holdings, were effective. And if the foundation of Riddle money was, by its vast size, essentially inviolate, Jamie was not.

"It's like playing chess with myself," Riddle told Max. His defenses were anticipated, his countermoves foreseen. He had tried to trace the phone calls and telegrams back to their source, "but he's thought of that one too."

By the end of the first week Riddle realized that the double had even begun moving within the main house itself. He heard that he had broken into Stella's game room and smashed her Dresden figurines. Soames reported seeing Jamie leave the house. "I heard the sound of breaking china," the man told Max. "I imagine it was about midnight. When I proceeded to investigate, I saw Mr. Riddle stalking from the room. I called to him. He said something unpleasant to me. Then he continued on his way. I believe he went out to the garden. I didn't see him return, although he called for his coffee this morning from his study."

"What was it he said to you?" They sat in the servants' lounge. Max had cornered Soames in the kitchen, and brought him there. Apparently he had already heard about the figurines ground to powder in the rug. Stella had been crying. She had not come out of her room.

"It was very unlike him, sir."

"I'm sure of that, Soames. I still want to know what it was he said."

Soames reddened. One hand was a tight fist. His head was rigid. He spoke to the wall, no longer looking at Max. He spoke quietly, no intonation. "He called me a cocksucker, sir, and he said that I was next. I don't believe that he's well."

"No. I'd be surprised if he was," Max muttered.

At the end of two weeks Riddle estimated that the double had been inside the house on at least four occasions. It had entered for short periods of time, but it had taken to moving about brazenly as a ghost. It no longer seemed to fear discovery. It took certain pains to ensure that it would never actually be seen in Riddle's presence, coming in back doors, staying in sections of the far wing that Riddle rarely visited, but it no longer remained unseen.

It had been cruel to the servants. Mrs. McGuire told how she had come into the small gallery in the far south quarters of the house and seen Jamie defacing a portrait of himself. The eyes of the painting had been smudged with black ink so they appeared to be empty dark sockets. When she spoke to him, he called her by name and said, "How would you like me to do this to your eyes?"

The next morning she handed in her resignation to Soames. He managed to change her mind with a rats-leaving-the-sinking-ship speech. She agreed to give it another few weeks.

Even after Riddle had ordered the locks changed on all doors, and posted guards at every corner with orders to let no one go unchallenged, the double managed to get by. "Sir, you told me

I was fired," a bewildered guard told Riddle.

"When?"

"Last night, sir. You came up the path, and I repeated your orders that no one was to be allowed entry. Then you told me I was fired, and let yourself in with my key."

It was a slow steady descent into a private hell for Jamie Riddle. He had again retreated to his study. He slept only intermittently. He ate poorly. His only counselor was Max, and Max too had begun to show signs of collapse. They both drank a great deal. Each morning the servants brought them food and found empty bottles at the door.

As a surprise to no one, Riddle became ill. The most salient symptom was a fever. It neither abated nor increased. He had refused medication, refused to see a doctor. After only three days with the fever he looked, quite literally, like death warmed over. And rumor had it, he had also taken to talking to himself.

Five floors up at the top of Swan's Way, alone, only a single pool of light in a cold study, rarely emerging, ruling like a spirit from the grave, no wonder there were rumors.

Some of them were fairly serious. A chambermaid told Max that she had heard the cook complaining. "He's gone mad up there, all alone, ranting to himself." Then Mrs. McGuire claimed she had heard Riddle cursing and pounding the walls. The next morning when she came to clean the room she saw that he had done an awful thing. "All the trophy heads that his father had brought from all over the world. All those beautiful mounted heads. The big moose head, the tiger, the deer. Why, he's taken the glass eyes out of every one of them. Why would he do a thing like that?"

Why the eyes, indeed? Riddle asked himself. He hardly remembered the act. It had been late. Not long before dawn. He had slept badly. Carry had once more tried to get him to talk, but he had nothing to say. Finally when she fell asleep he got out of bed and groped along the dark hall to the study. He remembered he hadn't been thinking clearly. In the blackness ordinary familiar things in the room had seemed to come alive.

An embroidered rose on a lampshade became a mouth with bared teeth. A pair of socks in the corner became rats, frozen with fear, but hunched and bristling and ready to attack. And if that weren't enough his thoughts had a life of their own. Time was compressed. A gallery of images, like a row of dominoes, began collapsing in on him. Some were disturbingly unrelated to anything; a baby he had once seen floating in a jar of formaldehyde; a pet turtle left in the sun too long. Other thoughts were to be expected: Toby's description of Eric's body; Candy's face. He had been strangely conscious of his hands. They were moving on their own accord again.

Sometime after he had gone into the study, and yet before he had found the light switch, so that it was still completely dark, he saw the face of the *doppelgänger*. It was as if it were floating in front of him . . . it was only in his mind. He struggled for the lights, knowing it would melt in the light. And then the lights were on and he was looking at eyes as lifeless and malevolent as the ones he'd just pictured. They were the eyes of his father's trophies. Tearing them out had been automatic. He had done it with the letter opener and, when the blade had snapped, with his hands.

Even the veneer of the prosaic evaporated. The normal observance of meals ceased. The teas with cakes and marmalade ended. Then without a word to Riddle, Stella left. She took Soames and the main of the help, leaving him only a skeleton staff. Michael, withdrawn into silent catatonia since he had seen Jamie, was moved to a clinic in Switzerland, and his mother and sister joined him.

They left in a pale afternoon. From the window in his study Riddle watched the stiff procession of black luggage being shuttled to the cars. He tapped a finger on the window as the cars pulled out. Goodbye.

Later that day Carry announced she was leaving too. Riddle found her packing in the bedroom. They had seen little of each other during the previous two weeks. By now it was as much from her avoidance as his negligence. She had a canvas suitcase on the bed and was throwing her clothing in like rags to the Goodwill bin. He asked her what she was doing and she said, "Leaving you."

"Why?"

"Why do you think? Jamie, nothing's working for us. I can't live this way. You're destroying yourself. You won't tell me what's wrong. You won't let me help, and I can't bear to watch it any longer."

"But I need you." He sounded pathetic. He knew it, but couldn't help it. His voice cracked. He tried to go on, then broke off in a fit of coughing.

"I'm sorry, but I can't make it here, Jamie. I'll come back when you get it together."

Now genuinely desperate. "Look, I'll handle it. I'll get it together. We can go away. We can go to the tropics. Bright sun, blue sea . . . goddamn you!"

"Jamie, come on. It's five in the afternoon and you're already drunk. You've been drinking all the time. You never talk to me. You look terrible. Max too. I can't tell which of you is worse off. I don't want to know anymore. I just want out."

There was a moment when he almost told her. She was crying. He saw her in the mirror. She wiped her eyes on the sleeve of her blouse. He saw his own reflection. There were dark circles around his eyes. They were bloodshot. His lips were dry and cracked. His clothes were wrinkled. The top two buttons of his shirt were missing. The cuffs hung loose. There were stains. It was the vision of himself and Carry that nearly put him over the edge. The last time he would see her? He thought it was very possibly true.

She crying, he a wreck, their reflections framed in an arabesque of gold filigree. The mirror reflects before throwing back an image, he remembered . . . And then he was really about to say it. He would tell her even though she would never understand. None of this was his own doing, he would say. There was a nightmare. It had broken through the wall of dreams, it had taken over his life. He was losing and he didn't know how to change it. It was lonely and he needed her and if she left him they would never see each other again.

He said nothing. Later he told Max that it was best that Carry not be around. The two men had entered the study. Max stood at a slouched attention. There were bags beneath his eyes. His hair was a wispy mess. The wrinkled shirt was buttoned to the top, but he wore no tie—like an immigrant trying his best to please the border guards. When he raised his eyes, Jamie caught a glimpse of dignity.

"And I want you to go too, Max. It's a long way past where you can help. It's going to be messy here." He was avoiding the eyes. "Look, I don't want you here. You'll make it harder for me . . . damn it, Max, you don't understand—"

"Yes I do, Jamie. I understand completely. I'm old. I know where my future is. There's nothing for me out there. This house, this room, these four walls, all the years are going to climax here. And I'm not really afraid, not anymore. I can't fight for you, but I can stay with you. I can talk to you. I can listen."

A few minutes later the two men were moving down the hall. Riddle put his arm around Max. Max made an innocent joke about the blind leading the blind. Then he told Jamie that he agreed it was good that Carry was gone. "Only now it changes things. Now that we're alone."

Riddle understood. He meant that the double was now entirely free to walk Swan's Way.

Room after room, past massive portraits in which glum faces glared through swirls of oyster-grey shadows, past landscapes beneath black ruptures of clouds, the double could move undisturbed. There were great rooms where dances were once held and the parquetry tiles were once showered with the light of thirteen chandeliers. Now these rooms were empty and dark. There were rooms where society was once entertained, lounging on tulipwood, palisander and satinwood commodes with ormolu mounts and terra-cotta statuettes, and these rooms were empty and dark too. There were wide, long halls where the clack of a footstep skittered off a glazed inlay floor that shone like glass and then rippled through seemingly acres of empty corridors. And later that night, when they were all gone,

Riddle heard those steps and went from room to room, throwing open doors, straining in the dark for the figure of himself, seeing no one.

He returned sweating and trembling and told Max, "We're beaten," then fell onto the leather couch. Max handed him a bottle of gin, and after two slugs he started to cough. Jamie told Max he could no longer think of what to do next. His words became garbled. There were some bloody flakes on his lower lip. His voice had been rising, the words spilling out in a ragged bark. He stopped. "I've got to get Carry out of here. He'll come after her next. I know it. I've got to get her to leave."

"Carry's already gone, Jamie," Max told him. "She left earlier this afternoon. She's gone to Europe."

Riddle stared at him stupidly. "I . . . I forgot. I don't remember her saying goodbye. Did she at least say that to me?"

Riddle began to wind his watch. The mechanism broke, but when Max left, he was still winding his watch.

Chapter 35

AT some point on the road Carry actually told herself that it was over. "I've lost him." She said this out loud, above the hum of the engine, above the radio. "I've lost him," and the tears began to roll down freely. Now she was simply putting distance between them. It was registering on her Triumph's speedometer, miles on top of miles. She was sailing through a blackened countryside. Headlights cut a long thin tunnel, rising and dipping with the highway. She once used to pretend that Jamie was her lover. That was when they were very young. Then he became her lover, and now she would have to pretend that he never was. When the radio turned to static there was nothing to keep her from thinking about him, and the grief was unbearable.

Once she'd told him that love was hating the same enemies. It had been a joke. He had just told her that he loved her because she wore a man's wristwatch. They had been out on a schooner, moored in San Francisco Bay. Jamie was on leave from whatever it was that he had been doing. The sun was an orange ball big as the eye of an egg. Green champagne bottles were floating out to sea with the tide. One had a message in it: "I love Carry, still." Silver lights, like the million candles of the faithful, were blowing out along the coast. "And what is love?"

"It's hating the same enemies," she had said.

She slid the gears into neutral and coasted to the side of the road. Trees and hedges that lined the highway were glowing in the spray of headlights. Then they started to blur with tears because the truth of the matter was, Jamie had an enemy and she had deserted him. Even though that enemy was himself, in their own private world leaving was the cardinal sin. Jamie was very ill, and she had deserted him. One could never pretend that hadn't happened. She had deserted him, and now she would never see him again. For as long as they lived they would both remember and she would never be able to ask him to love her.

When they had separated years ago, love was still always possible. It bound them together, and in a way forced them apart. Jamie wanted to run off to a war, or hire on a ship. He was supposed to return with a vial of sand from Byzantium, a pouch of looted gold and a gentleman's waistcoat with buttons of real ivory. He was supposed to return tanned from the tropics, maybe even scarred from battle with savages. Then Swan's Way would fall at his feet. They would live together in that castle, and finally there would be no enemies because Jamie had killed them all.

But something went wrong. Carry was not sure what. It had something to do with the extremes that real hate had driven him to. He had charged after ghosts, spirits really. He had gone hunting the evil spirit of wealth and greed. He went off to battle all the phantoms that had haunted him as a boy, all the arrogance of a society of the privileged, all the double standards, and most of all the evil that he believed ran through the veins of them all . . . himself included.

In the end, perhaps, those spirits offered no resistance. Perhaps there had been nothing to fight. But when Jamie finally realized this, it was already very late. He had already become a warrior, and when no enemy came forward to fight, he invented one. And even if that wasn't the whole truth, the fact remained that Jamie was very ill. There was something inside him that was tearing him apart. One could kiss and say goodbye a thousand times and still one would never forget. And in the end it was love, and the pain of a love that would never be forgotten no matter how many miles she put between them, that made Carry turn the car around and head back to Jamie.

"The double holds the most horrible truth." Ten years ago that had meant little to Max. Another old German proverb. He had come across thousands of them. And that one in particular, so nasty and so German, had always reminded him of Hitler's eleventh-hour battle cry, "And now I hold the most horrible weapon!"

However, there was more to the proverb. Of course the double holds the most horrible truth. That went without saying. But now in the face of defeat Max was beginning to understand, beginning to realize just how deep it went.

Max had not admitted defeat. Not to Jamie, not really even to himself. He was tired, that's all. He felt dead tired, and he padded off to his bedroom. He had assured himself that in the morning Jamie would know what to do. They would both have the strength to fight in the morning, but now he had to sleep.

It had gone on too long. There had been no rest for too long. He was dizzy. He felt as if he were witnessing life from the wrong end of a telescope. When Jamie would speak to him, the voice seemed to be coming from miles away. He had trouble understanding even the simplest things. It was as if they had spun off the edge of the world and for two weeks had been floating in a void, like the hazy malaise after a long fever. And Jamie's fever had still not broken. He was wasting away, burning slowly. They both needed sleep.

For Max, the symptoms were similar. His vision had gone bad. Small coincidences suddenly seemed to have great meaning. It frightened him. Even just walking down the corridor to his room, locking the door, finding that his bed, the walls, the carpets, everything had that dirty unwell tinge to it.

But then he lay down and closed his eyes and, suddenly, it was a taste of heaven. He felt as if he were falling, very slowly falling, head over heels through a cool, placid sea. Images, faces he had known from years ago, snatches from an old tune about sailing ships, they drifted past him like leaves in an October wind. He felt lovely and safe, and so even when he heard that voice he wasn't disturbed . . . "The double holds the most horrible truth" . . . Nothing really so malicious about it. It was gentle, like the voice of a preacher laying down the last rites. When he sang it over in his mind, for the first time he knew that it was true. He couldn't understand how that line had never made sense to him before. Because there was the double standing over him. Its eyes were vacant. If that was the reflection of the worst in a human being, then it was true . . . "The double held the most horrible truth . . ."

The double laid open Max's throat with one stroke of a straight razor. Max tried to scream. What came out was blood. The last that he saw were those eyes, and the last that he came to understand was why Jamie had torn out the eyes of his father's trophies. They had been of glass. They mocked life. Just like the eyes of the double.

He was fully aware of the hand he was dealing. The years of the hunt were winding down to minutes. Terror was revenge, Swan's Way the spoils. He had walked back through the forest. He had kept low under the brush to avoid the guards. "This is my new home," he had told himself. "This will be the last time I enter here like a thief."

There was Swan's Way, like a fallen castle. It was dark and empty, except for the yellow glow of two or three lights where the wolf lay panting. Rows of blank windows seemed to rise up to the clouds. The great wings rolled out across the lawn. "Tonight what belongs to me will be mine," he said. Terror had won the easiest victory. . . .

Climbing the stairs he had heard voices. The wolf had been ranting. Max, the fat one, had been listening. Then the voices had stopped. There had been footsteps plodding above. The fat one was going to his room. He was locking his door. He was on his bed.

Ten minutes later his throat was torn out.

Now the slut. Must kill her, but slowly, he admonished himself. Kill her with pain so that the wolf will understand, a small repayment for all his stolen life . . .

Except she was gone. She was not in her room. She may have been with the wolf in the study because he hadn't yet checked the study. He wasn't quite ready for the wolf yet. He wanted the wolf to wake up and know what it was like to be completely alone. Alone like I was alone for all those years. The wolf was going to die with full comprehension that he would be alone until the end of time.

He moved from room to room, empty and dark. Even most of the servants were gone, and those that had stayed lay huddled asleep. He passed a window that overlooked the drive and acres of lawn in the moonlight. Beyond was the forest and— driving up was . . .

Her.

The wolf must have been flat out on his back, because he hadn't even seen his beloved drive up. Didn't even hear the engine. So it was left to the new master of the house to meet the lady on the steps of his estate.

Carry ran to him and fell into his arms. She kissed him and told him everything was going to be all right. He said yes it was. Then she started to lead him up the steps but he said, "No, let's go into the garden house where we can be alone, where it's quiet." They walked arm in arm. She clung to him and told him she loved him. He kissed her and whispered, "Hush."

Inside the garden house he laid her on the velvet settee. When he turned on a single light she said she preferred the dark, but he answered, "I want to be able to see you." Actually he wanted her to be able to see him . . . when the time was right and he had broken her like a swallow's egg, he wanted her to see his face and know that he was not the wolf. And she would know it from his eyes . . .

He told her how it was true that everything was going to be

all right. He said that he had had some bad dreams, but now everything was under control. "We can go away, and have a real life together." He talked about places he knew in the south seas where the white scalloped sand was printless for miles. They would live in a house cut of palm leaves with the shell of a pearly nautilus for the knocker on a driftwood door. "I love you," he said. He brushed a blond strand of hair from her face. "They say that money can't buy love, and it's true. Love is the only hint of immortality. When we die we are sent to a place where it's cold and lonely. We are sent to a desert with only sand and rock. Cold rock and flat cracked earth from one horizon to the other. We come from there, and we have to return there. Maybe with love we can go someplace else. I want to believe we can. I want to believe it very much . . ."

He kissed her, first lightly, then more forcefully. She stirred. His fingers peeled away the silk of her blouse. His lips went to her breast, first with kisses, then softly nibbling, and finally a little harder. She pressed him into her body, his mouth still at her breast. Now he was biting harder. "Jamie, that hurts." He slid a hand up to her throat, and his teeth drew blood. She screamed but his hand was at her throat and choked it off. She began to struggle, only now his hands were like iron claws. "Please!" It was barely a whimper. He pulled his hand away. She gasped for breath. "Jamie, why? Jamie . . . Jamie!" He slapped her across the mouth.

"I'm not your Jamie, you bitch!" And when she tried to scream he slapped her again.

And again.

Chapter 36

RIDDLE fell out of sleep. Something had happened. It was his first impression and it washed over him like ice water. Something had passed him by. Yes, the double had come . . . he could almost smell it. It had come, struck and he'd been asleep. Not even asleep, he had been unconscious. He pressed a hand against his eyes. He held it, and oh yes, this was rock bottom all right. He and Max had finally found it, rock bottom in the old Twilight Zone. Where was Max?

He stumbled down the hall. Ahead was the door to Max's bedroom. He was like a camera recording the converging stream of carpet and white plaster in the gloom. He saw the door ajar, and then there was a surge of nausea. It really was like a film. He was in the bedroom, seeing it all for the second time. First Candy, now Max. He sagged against the door jamb. "He's only sleeping," he whispered inanely. "Max," he whispered again. And then, finally, came the scream. And when the scream was gone, used up, there was only a small voice that said, "Ah, Max, no."

As he slumped to the floor, his hand dragged down the wall and hit the light switch and he saw the blood and Max's eyes wide, vacant.

At some point he realized that he was crying into a vacuum of stillness. Everything was stockstill. The crickets, the mockingbirds. There was not a breath of wind. He imagined that even the clocks had stopped. The hour of the noonday devil? Of course not, it was night. Then the hour of the wolf? Maybe, but it was something else. Something had just come into the room. Not the double, nothing with flesh and blood. A ghost, the ghost of Radan, and the old bastard thinks he can help. Well, it wasn't really Radan's ghost, or at least not ghost as in dead people. Radan was Old Testament. He would probably live past a hundred. But, no question, something of Radan had just come into the room. He could even hear it speak to him. It was telling him that it was tired of his sad pitiful performance. It was telling him to reach down inside himself and drag out what was born the day he had killed Erhart. Rip it out, it told him. Rip it out and hold it to your face. Study it, look at it, understand it, love it, and then swallow it again and this time let it grow inside you.

"And what's that supposed to be?" Riddle asked.

"Why, it's a kind of rage," Radan told him, and for the first time that Riddle could remember, Radan was smiling.

Riddle was staring into the mirror above the dresser beside the bed, where Max's body lay. Rage? His head was cocked, listening. Yes, it was true. Something had just entered his body. It had come all the way up from hell. Radan was right, the thing that was in him now was a kind of rage, but a rage that was changing him, turning him into somebody else.

" 'Somebody else'? " Radan challenged. "Somebody else! It's you, Jamie. It's *you.* "

And Radan was right again, because now he was the monster, not Radan's monster but his own. The monster was angry, very angry. It had been primed for one thing: to kill.

"Is this far enough down the road?" Riddle asked.

"Oh, easily so," Radan had to answer.

"Are you ready?" Radan had once asked. Riddle had held out his hand and Radan could see that he hadn't been. "I've given you technique," Radan had told him, and that, of course, was the speed of his hand and his knowledge of weapons. But technique was like wealth. It had given power, but the power wasn't absolute. "As evil is absolute," Radan said. "Evil is the mirror of good." Radan had told him that time and time again, but Riddle hadn't understood. Or refused to.

Once Radan had asked Riddle, "After you killed Erhart in the wood, how did you feel?"

"You mean, after Erhart was dead?"

"Yes, after he was dead."

"I felt frightened."

Of course he felt frightened . . . Who wouldn't have been? One moment there was little Jamie, rich punk, tough guy, and then the next moment there was the monster. There was no middle ground with that beast. It got mad, and then killed. There were no second thoughts, no existential bullshit. That monster wasn't any romantic rebel. It didn't muck around. The thing went right for the throat. . . .

Now, still before his mirror, Riddle was looking right into the monster's face.

"Terrible, isn't it?" Radan was saying. Riddle nodded, and Radan told him, "Well, go ahead, admit it. *Admit it.*"

"It's me," Riddle said very quietly. "It isn't someone else, it's me."

Radan worshipped before a God that killed the first born of every family, only passing by the houses with the mark of blood. Radan's God turned sticks into cobras, spat out plagues of locusts, drowned the world in water, and then turned the water to blood. His God didn't turn the other cheek. He was a vengeful God. Radan's God was the model for what Radan had made of Riddle. Radan's God killed people. The Devil himself had nothing on this monster created by Radan. The monster had been made in the image of God.

The double was evil, unmitigated evil, Riddle understood now as he strode off down the hallway. He wanted to tell him that . . . that he finally knew him.

He was moving like a panther, slipping in and out between the rows of violets and roses. It was out there, and before he even began to consider how he would find it, how he would kill it, he saw the light in the garden house.

Inside, Carry was tied to the bed. There was a rag in her mouth and rope around her neck. Whenever her whimpers and moans threatened to break into screams, the double would pull on the rope and cut them off. Twice she had lost consciousness but he was patient. There was nothing he wanted her to do but suffer. Nothing he wanted her to confess. This was not an inquisition. This was merely torture, and Carry was nearly insane with the pain.

Then the door was open and the double saw that the wolf had come, and it was a wolf who knew the truth.

Riddle stood in the doorway, breathing hard. Carry saw him. Her eyes went wide, first from the double, then to Riddle, back and forth. Her head began to loll from side to side. She mumbled under the gag. Riddle ignored her. His eyes, burning bright, were only for the double.

Like a wolf, the double thought. He's crazed . . . like a wolf. The double brought the knife up, red hot from being held in the flame of a candle. It had been effective with the girl, but now it was useless. Riddle kicked it away, swung wide and caught the double in the ribs. The double went crashing through the furniture and struck the wall. Stunned, he was up again. He'd had no idea that the wolf could have ever managed such strength. He still wasn't beaten, though.

They moved in on one another, wavering, circling, opposite ends of the same identity, locked into the dance of a final rendezvous. The double lunged, kicking out, but when he dipped to swing his leg he also grabbed the poker from the fireplace. Riddle took the blow at the shoulder and rode the pain back to the wall. The double was advancing on him now, the poker hissing through the air, sweeping in wide arcs.

Riddle knew the alternatives. He could avoid the poker, try to strike between the cuts. Which was the expected. Move in, let the double bring that poker down, dodge and then swing. That would be the logical way, because one good blow from the poker could end things. But if Riddle could take the blow and survive, absorb it as he had done with the first one, then the double would be open.

He moved in. The double, expecting him to withdraw, hesitated for an instant. Riddle did not withdraw. The poker came down, aimed for the head. Riddle managed to twist, and it struck his back. The force snapped him into an arch and off balance. If the double hit him again he'd go down, but Riddle was moving very quickly. He took the pain, used it to fuel him. It was propelling him forward. His hand was a steel claw. It reached for the double's groin, grabbed, twisted. The double screamed and went down on his knees. Riddle wrenched him to his feet, grabbing him by the hair. The double was going through the air, and the wall exploded in his face.

A roar in his ears, blood in his mouth. Something slammed into his shoulder, like a giant hammer. It was Riddle's fist, and it snapped the double's arm at the elbow. He tried a wild swing with his good arm. Riddle caught it, twisted the wrist back until it cracked. The double fell to his knees.

Riddle paused. He was half-crouched, swaying a bit from side to side, like a cobra. "You shouldn't do this to me," the double was saying . . . "we're the same, we need each other, I'm your other half, we've come from the same—" Riddle's leg had shot out, slamming it in the stomach.

Flat out, face down, the double wheezed blood. "You don't understand . . . I'm you and you're me . . . we're one man . . ." Its voice was strangely high, almost mellifluous. "You need me, I need you . . . no brothers close as we are . . ." The words were coming out in gentle, murmuring sighs. He could hear the girl's muffled sobs, Riddle's deep regular breath, the faint gurgling sound in his own chest . . . "We've come so far for one another," he said, "traveled through different worlds, across cold space and now that we've met you can't end it this way, you can't leave me like this, have no right to leave me alone, I can't, not alone again, not alone . . ." Its cheek was pressed against the floor, mouth opening and shutting in a pool of blood.

Riddle bent down close to its face. "You're wrong. You look like me but"—a quick glance to Radan who nodded his approval—"but I can *see* you now, and you're not me. I can really see you, see you." He took a handful of its hair and pulled the face up to his. "Just like mine," he whispered for the last time, and smashed the double's face into the floor. Again and again, with every bit of strength he had. And when the double was finally dead, the face was an unrecognizable pulp.

For Carry there were only sporadic moments of clarity. Much of the night would come back to her in warped, distorted slices of memory, like the frames of a film projected too quickly. But still, as in any smear of experience, like accidents, or rapid travel through strange countries, there was a subliminal knowledge of the truth.

She knew that something important had happened. The facade of existence had somehow split open and she had seen a gross flaw. Jamie, pushed into one corner by the force that had driven him to extremes, had suddenly popped up in another.

So, there had been two of them. That much she would never forget. Even if she could not understand it, she would never forget it. One of them was not really Jamie, but there were also moments when neither of them was. At least not the Jamie she'd loved. The first was an animal. She remembered the hot knife, the pain, his fingers on her body. She remembered his garbled ongoing prattle as he hurt her . . . "So you're his bitch, little pretty bitch, little she-wolf . . . we're a pretty pair, a pretty team . . ."

Then there was the other one, the one that had come through the door like . . . She hardly knew how to describe it. He was charged with an unfathomable rage, a brutality, but at the same time there was something transcendent about it. He was like an angry god, and there was a kind of undeniable splendor in his fury.

Watching him move about the room, he seemed to be moving on some other plane. Graceful, in a way even beautiful. When his hands swung and feet kicked, the rest of his body adjusted with perfect fluidity, like a jellyfish gliding through deep water. The speed seemed to stop time. She remembered that he had wrapped her in a spread of lace that had covered the settee, then carried her outside and laid her on the grass.

The grass was cool and moist, and the dew soaked through the lace. He left her there, and when she saw him again he was toting a can of gasoline up the steps into the garden house.

Now, on the steps again, Carry saw a droplet of light spring from his fingers. Then another. Matches, she realized. He must have splashed the gasoline all over the garden house, because one of the matches caught and there was a bud of flame. The bud became an exploding blossom. The entire garden lit up. She saw him coming toward her, etched against a sheet of fire, like a phoenix sailing at her from the sun.

In the end it was like a dream. He was with her again, kneeling on the grass. She reached out and laced her fingers about his neck. When he rose, she was curled in his arms. Behind them, the timbers cracked in flames.

Tomorrow there would be nothing left but ashes. And so it was like a dream after all. Carry was left with only quiet impressions: herself in Jamie's arms, Jamie treading slowly over the lawn, the whispering brush of his footsteps through the leaves, the beat of his heart.